BAYOU REFUGE

JOSHUA POWELL

BAYOU REFUGE

AUTHOR'S NOTE

Please note that this work is intended as fiction. Writing has always been one of my passions—one I've usually kept to myself. However, this is a story I feel led to share. The aim was to grab the imagination of the reader through some fascinating fictional devices and then share how important the Gospel of Jesus Christ really is. The hope is that this encourages readers to ensure that they've placed their faith and trust in Jesus for salvation. It's also intended as a reminder that we never know when our next conversation with someone may be the last time they hear about the amazing love and hope found in Jesus Christ. Thank you for reading. If you enjoy it, please consider sharing a copy of it with someone else.

PROLOGUE

Charles finished his morning prayer, then opened his eyes and put his large study Bible on the small table next to his red leather recliner. He took a sip of black coffee from his favorite blue mug and looked out of the large glass window. A bit of light finally broke through the fog and illuminated the large Magnolia tree that was now in full bloom, and he could see a squirrel chasing another across the branches. A couple of birds flew away, perhaps annoyed by the squirrels. Charles hated the thought of having to drive in the fog, but he really wanted to get to the meeting this morning. He had missed the last one and felt badly about it. As pastor, his congregation did expect him to stay up to date with what was happening in their denomination.

Behind him, he could hear stirrings in the house. Deborah, his wife, was walking behind him down the hallway that led into the kitchen to fix herself a cup of tea. Connor, his sixteen-year-old son, walked into the living room and gave him a slight nod, then collapsed his bedhead onto the couch, scrambling for the remote to turn the television on. No doubt he was going to put on another nature documentary.

It seemed like all his son had ever wanted to watch from a young age were shows about wildlife. Charles didn't complain though. There were much worse things that Connor could want to watch.

"Mom, I can't find my hairbrush!" Shelby, his thirteen-year-old daughter, yelled from the hallway bathroom.

"That's because you left it on your dresser!" Deborah yelled back.

"Oh, yeah."

"How do you know that?" Connor chimed in. "That's not normal."

"It seems like I'm the only one in this house who knows where most things are, Connor. It must be a mom superpower!"

Connor looked at Charles for more of an explanation. Charles simply shrugged his shoulders, so Connor turned his head back to the television and selected a program about a zoo. Charles grabbed his cell phone from the small table next to his recliner and yanked the charger out. To his aggravation, the phone had not charged at all and was still dead, even though he had plugged it in an hour ago.

"Man, why won't this thing charge?"

"Because it's old and you need a new one," Connor replied.

"I don't need a new one. I just need to figure out how to make this one work. You don't need something new just because what you have gets a little old."

"A little old," Connor said with a laugh. "You got that phone when I was like eight. It's time to let go, Dad."

Charles hated the thought of throwing something out just because it was old. He knew he could get it charging again; it just needed the right touch, he'd done it numerous times. He got up and walked into the kitchen just in time to see Shelby sitting next to her mother at a small table for four. She was eating a bowl of cereal while Deborah sipped her tea. The two looked so much alike. They both had long brown hair and a few freckles on their cheeks, but Deborah's hair was not quite as full as Shelby's. They also both gave Charles the same half grin when he cracked a lame joke.

"You're not going to that meeting, are you?" Deborah asked.

"I need to. I missed the last one. Plus, the fog will clear in a bit."

"Just wait for it to clear, then leave." Deborah locked eyes with Charles in a way that indicated she was serious. "It's not just the fog that I'm worried about. You know a bad storm went through there a couple of days ago. I promise you that road hasn't been cleared properly. Those parish crews don't get in a rush for anything. Mark my words, there'll be a wreck today."

"I'll take it slow, but I need to get on the road so I can get there in time. Stop worrying. I've got it under control. You know Mrs. Hebert and her crew are going to want to know what's going on with the ladies' ministry, and that report is up first."

"First of all, I don't think she'd want you driving through God knows what to get there. Secondly, I don't really care what she wants. I'm your wife, and I don't want you to go. Besides, can't you just join the meeting online or something? Do you have to be there? What year are we living in now?" Deborah replied firmly.

Charles thought about the possibility of letting the fog clear before he left, while Deborah's eyes still pleaded with him not to go. However, he didn't want to let his congregation down and was sure that there was nothing to worry about.

"I'll be fine," Charles said, then leaned in to kiss his wife on the cheek, who did nothing to return the affection. He hugged his daughter, yelled goodbye to Connor, and headed out the door.

CHAPTER 1

Charles hated the fog. The South Louisiana roads were already bad enough on a clear day, but avoiding potholes and bumps in the fog added yet another unnecessary obstacle. Then there were the intersections. Sure, the old country roads had stop signs. But it wasn't like anyone paid much attention to them when they were in a hurry. Leaving the house with Deborah upset was weighing heavily on him. As a pastor's wife, Deborah had been there with Charles many times when he'd ministered to families who had been through traumatic events, including one of Deborah's closest friends, whose husband died in a car accident on a bridge during a thunderstorm. Charles could appreciate why she was upset, but she needed to realize that he still had a job to do. Like it or not, today it meant driving through the fog.

As a younger man, Charles would have never hesitated or given much thought to his wife's warning, but he was getting closer to forty-five, and his eyesight wasn't what it used to be. After a half hour of driving through thick fog, he wondered if Deborah was right, though it was hard for him to admit defeat. Still, he hated to miss a meeting he was expected to be attending. So he rubbed his salt-and-pepper goatee and mustache, adjusted his glasses, took a sip of black coffee from his metal coffee cup, and refocused himself. He had planned for a longer drive given the autumn fog that this area was notorious for, and all that was left to do was to endure it.

Charles tried to focus on someone on the radio who talking about the events leading up to World War II, but as much as he loved history, and as passionate as the announcer was about that war, Charles's mind kept turning to other things. He thought about Connor's successful summer ball season. He knew that his son would probably never be a professional ball player, but still, he was so proud of the way he had worked hard to improve his overall game. He was turning out to be quite the second baseman. Then there was the mission project that Connor had organized with his team to help provide relief supplies to hurricane victims. Connor had even given up two weekends to go and help clean out the homes of those impacted. He was also proud of Shelby, who was in seventh grade. It constantly impressed him how smart she was. She'd ask him complicated questions about everything from science, to history, to the nature of God. As a pastor, the last one really impressed him. He never thought he'd have those kinds of conversations with someone so young. He was blessed and tried to count those blessings and thank God for them regularly.

On foggy mornings like this, the predictably monotonous drive became much more challenging to navigate. Even trying to figure out exactly where he was on a highway he had traveled through at least a couple of times a year was not easy. In order to make sure he didn't miss a turn, he turned a quick glance to his phone sitting in a holder on the dashboard and noticed the battery light was red, but the phone was not on yet. He fiddled with the charger cord for a moment, but it still wasn't charging. He could hear Connor's voice in his head. *Dad, quit being so cheap and buy a new cell phone.* Even as a pastor of a small church, he needed a phone he could rely on, and his six-year-old iPhone was not cutting it. Realizing that not only was Deborah correct in her concern for his safety in the fog, but also that Connor was right in his urging him to get a new phone was aggravating. He liked being in control and struggled with admitting when he was wrong. With little visibility, he might miss the next turn. Charles sighed heavily. He was really going to be struggling with directions now. He kept trying to adjust the cord, hoping it would pick up a charge. *How can it not be charging at all? Maybe the cord is bad?* Perhaps he should have stayed home. After several more failed attempts, he made up his mind to stop at a gas station in a few minutes to let the fog clear a bit and buy another charger. He looked down at his nearly empty coffee cup and thought a refill wouldn't hurt either.

Then it happened: the phone screen flashed briefly, then went blank again. He looked for road markers in the fog, but this wasn't a road he drove down often. Still, it cut through several small towns he had been to for various events over the years. After several minutes he spotted a familiar faded sign for an approaching community store that, although closed for several years, indicated the community was only a few miles away. There was a combination gas station and deli there that had pretty good coffee. He was still ahead of schedule and figured he could get the phone charged if he had a few minutes to put his full focus on it. His frustration began to ease. In a few minutes everything would be okay; there was nothing to worry about.

Charles had lost signal on the radio station he was listening to so he tried to find a new station, but the knob in his old Camry fell into his hand. Another painful reminder that he was, at times, too cheap. He turned his eyes down for a moment to reattach the knob . . . then felt a sickening thud. His whole body shook, and the force made his eyes shut for a split second. He quickly applied the brakes and put on his emergency flashers, thinking he'd run over something. He saw a turnoff into a sugarcane field and drove fifty feet or so to get his car off the main road, then turned the engine off. Unsure of what had really happened, Charles tried to calm his racing heart as his adrenaline spiked. He looked down at his slightly faded red dress shirt and khakis, not sure what he was expecting to see but wanting to make sure that he was unharmed. Then he lifted a hand up to adjust his glasses only to realize both his hands were trembling—almost uncontrollably. He took a few deep breaths until his hands calmed slightly. As he looked into the rearview mirror, he was unable to see anything but himself and the thick fog.

"What was that?" he said, alarmed and confused.

He stepped outside of the car onto the damp grass and thick, wet mud, which stuck to the bottom of his black dress shoes and made loud suction noises. Normally, this would have aggravated him beyond measure, but he was too distracted at the moment. He walked toward the edge of the road and paused, then walked back toward the car, still disoriented. Suddenly, he saw the Camry shake. Seconds later, the ground under him shook too. Snaps, swooshes, and a final loud thump followed. Still seeing hazily through the fog, Charles realized what had happened. A large tree limb had fallen while he was driving, which he had run over. The size of it made his stomach drop. Then the entire tree had followed suit and collapsed too. Thankfully, he'd driven his car—and himself—to safety! But running over a limb that size should have wreaked havoc on the Camry, and could have even flipped the car. Charles was lucky to be alive. Tears began to form as he chided himself for looking away from the road to put the radio dial back on. He had told his kids the dangers of not paying attention for even seconds countless times, but hadn't listened to his own advice. Lost in his thoughts, he walked around uneasily, trying to process the scene, then realized he was standing in the middle of the road.

"Come on, Charles. Get it together," he mumbled as he moved to the side of the road.

"God, I'm so sorry!" Charles cried out. "Forgive me for not paying attention. Thank You for keeping me safe." He walked to the car to assess the damage his vehicle had endured in the incident. Given the size of the branch, he was expecting some pretty good dings. However, the vehicle looked unharmed with the exception of the previous "character marks" it had, given its advanced age. He stood there for a moment and tried to process everything. Ultimately, though, all he could do was mutter another prayer of thanks to God for taking care of him.

He looked down at his hands and noticed how filthy they were, then remembered that his gym bag was in the trunk. He popped it open and found some wipes and a towel.

He cleaned his hands and then and sat down in the driver's seat to get the mud off his shoes when he heard a very unexpected noise.

His cell phone was ringing.

CHAPTER 2

The ringing of Charles's phone caught him off guard. *It was dead, right?* He pondered how weird this was for a second before looking at the phone to see what the caller ID said: "Davy Collins." Davy was his denomination's retiring regional director. But last he had heard, Davy was active in title only. His assistant director had taken over because Davy, as of a few months ago, had begun to show some signs of a fast-acting type of Alzheimer's.

"This is strange," Charles said to no one in particular, but he answered anyway. "Hey, Davy. How are you?"

"Better than ever," Davy's deep, joyous voice replied. Charles had noticed that during the last several conversations he'd had with Davy, there had been a sense of confusion in his voice, almost as if he was second-guessing everything he was saying. It was heartbreaking, because Davy was a military veteran and had always conveyed such confidence even in challenging times. So to see his friend shaken and confused was hard to process. However, Charles couldn't hear that confusion in his voice now. As he looked out into the fog, he smiled, relieved to hear the voice of his old friend and mentor again. "How are you this morning, Charles?"

"To be honest, Davy, not so great. I've been struggling in this fog to get to the meeting. Carter said he's got a big announcement, and we're excited to hear it, but I managed to run over a fallen tree branch on the way up here. Honestly, it scared the living daylights out of me. It was so foggy I didn't even know what I had hit. I had to pull over and figure out what had happened."

"I've told you for a while now, if you're going to drive these Louisiana backroads, you need something a little bigger than that old car you've got. Are you okay?" Davy asked.

"I think so. Just a little shook up. But I'm about to head on to the meeting. You sound good. Last I heard you were really struggling. What's on your mind this morning?" Charlie tried his best to hide his confusion about why Davy called.

"Well, Martha keeps all my meds and stuff straight. Sometimes the doctors change it up a bit. I'm all right, I guess. Where are you at right now?"

"Not too far from Golder," Charles said, feeling like maybe Davy was trying to avoid the question. "Still about an hour out, maybe a little longer with this fog."

"Well, I'll save you some time and tell you what is going on. We're reopening Bayou Refuge."

Charles thought about this for a moment. He was surprised by the news, but part of him was encouraged to hear it. Bayou Refuge had been a special retreat center their denomination had run for years. The place was situated on a slightly higher elevation than the surrounding area, which was generally flat. The result of this height was that during certain times of the year, you almost felt like you were on an island with the bayou behind you and the river before you. Bayou Refuge had a few rustic cabins out there and an old library with a tremendous amount books. None were very up to date, but they had all of the classics of the Christian faith. There was a small dining area, probably no bigger than a small coffee shop, and a few small conference rooms. The area had some nice fishing spots as well as a few pavilions and uncovered seating areas with views reminding a peace-filled viewer that God masterfully designed and created the natural world. Over the years, churches held staff retreats there, ministers would sneak away to refresh and spend some time studying God's Word and praying, and smaller churches hosted special events on the property.

However, what Bayou Refuge had become famous for over the years were the Seeker Retreats. Seeker Retreats were free events open to the public. Anyone could sign up to stay in a cabin, have access to the library, and sit with a minister one on one daily and ask questions about God or the Bible. Pastors in their region would take turns being the host for these events. The groundskeeper and his wife would prepare the meals for the guests and the pastor, as well as taking care of any needed cleaning. Charles had been a part of dozens of these in years past, but it had been ten years since Bayou Refuge had been open. Every year at the annual meeting, since Bayou Refuge's closing, there had been intense discussion on selling the facility. However, they hadn't been able to find an interested buyer.

"Really, Davy? That's great news. I always loved that place. When is it going to reopen?"

"Well, I'm out here now. We're gonna host the first Seekers Retreat this weekend. And I want you to host it," Davy said.

"What?" Charles said, louder than he meant to, questioning his old friend's mental state. "Kind of sudden, isn't it? Davy, that would mean I'd need to be out that way tomorrow. I don't know if I can pull that off."

"Well . . ." Davy said with a bit of a chuckle. "Actually, I'd need you out here today."

"There's no way I can do that. Deborah's got a thing lined up with her sister this weekend, and there's a movie I've been telling the kids I would take them to see. Plus, I'd have to go to the meeting, then go home and get clothes, and then drive all the way out there. I'm sorry, Davy, maybe next weekend."

"You have to do this," Davy said with a loving but firm tone that felt like a general telling a trusted solider he had a mission that had to be done.

The strangeness in Davy's voice stirred Charles, almost as if he was compelled by God Himself and had no choice in the matter.

"I'm technically your superior here for just a little while longer, and I know this is where you need to be. I've known you for a long time, Charles, and I bet there's a gym bag in your vehicle with a change of clothes. Plus, you've probably got an emergency change of pants and a dress shirt in your trunk in case you ever have to leave somewhere unexpectedly and go to the hospital to pray with one of your church members. Am I right?"

Charles hated that Davy knew him so well. It also didn't sound like something that someone who was not in their right frame of mind would say. "You are right. I've got the emergency overnight bag."

"Everything else you need is at Bayou Refuge. They've got extra toothbrushes, all the toiletries, refreshments, and everything else. You just head on this way. I'll make a few phone calls and have someone lined up to cover your duties at the church for you," Davy said.

Charles reluctantly accepted the fact that he was going even though he had a million reasons not to. Then he remembered the problems he was having with his phone. "Davy, my phone has been on the fritz lately. Do you still have Deborah's number?"

"Yeah, sure. I'll give her a call and let her know what's going on. I know her and the kids will understand. It's gonna be an important weekend, Charles. I'll see you in a little while."

The call ended, and before Charles could decide if he was going to try to call Deborah or just let Davy handle it, the phone's screen flashed and went dead again. *How odd?*

Charles looked out into the sugarcane field. The fog still rested on everything like a thick, heavy blanket. He was almost certain he heard a siren in the background, then strained his head to try and hear it again. Nothing. It had gone silent.

But he uttered a short prayer that God would take care of whoever was hurt if that was the case. He started his Camry and pulled back onto the road, trying to remember the best route to Bayou Refuge.

CHAPTER 3

Charles continued to push through the fog after remembering which road he'd need to turn down. If he recalled correctly, he was only about forty-five minutes away from Bayou Refuge. The distance wasn't that far, but closer to the retreat center were several long and winding dirt roads—some of them one lane. Hopefully, the signs leading the way to the camp were still intact. It would be easy in this fog to make a wrong turn and wind up as lost as a goose in a snowstorm.

One thing was certain: there was a large part of Charles that didn't want to go. It was so sudden and so out of the blue that he couldn't believe his new plans were really in place. Last he had heard, Davy was making no day-to-day decisions and hadn't been into the office, even for a visit, in several months. But today? Seemed like he was calling all the shots. Something there didn't add up. He knew Deborah would want him to serve the Lord and honor those over him, but he figured she would also be pretty perplexed by this. Deborah was a very strong, independent woman who supported Charles and his desire to serve God without question—most of the time. However, Deborah's parents didn't have a great relationship, and growing up her dad was gone more than he was home. She had seen her mom struggle, functioning like a single mom even though she was technically married. Deborah had shared with him about the many nights growing up, lying in bed and hearing her mom sobbing because she felt so lonely. When Charles took long trips or had to leave unexpectedly, this would bring back those feelings of loneliness and abandonment for Deborah. Suddenly, he felt angry at himself over their interaction with each other this morning. Charles fussed at himself for not being more understanding and for not getting a new phone like she'd asked. If he had, she could hear from him about the change in plans instead of hearing it from Davy. The only thing keeping him from turning around and going home was this strange urge, one like he had never experienced before, making him feel like he had no real choice in the matter. In fact, he couldn't turn around and go home even if he tried.

"God, what is going on? Why do you have me going here? I'm so confused," Charles prayed. He stared out into the fog, waiting for some sort of answer. Not that he expected God's voice to come through the radio, but he often felt God's nudging, or heard a Bible verse in his mind, or had some other sort of confirmation when he asked a question like this to his Creator. As he came to the road he was supposed turn on, he felt a sense of calm and peace fall over him. It was so powerful that it almost brought a tear to his eyes. "Okay, God. If this is what you want me to do, I'll trust you. Just please take care of Deborah and the kids, and watch over the church while I'm away."

Charles continued his journey, reflecting on his new sense of peace. He took a quick glance at the digital clock on the dash and noticed that it was 8:00 a.m. He realized that the road was unusually empty, not that he expected a bunch of traffic. But there were plenty of homes scattering the side of the road, and he expected to see some folks out and about. The lack of activity felt a bit strange. However, the absence of other travelers did make the drive a little safer. The fog was also lifting a little, letting him see far enough ahead to feel confident driving the speed limit, which on this road was only thirty-five miles an hour.

He found a radio station playing old hymns, though he usually listened to stuff a bit more modern. With everything that had gone on this morning, he appreciated hearing these old songs of the faith, like "Victory in Jesus," "Softly and Tenderly," and "Love Lifted Me." They seemed to really resonate with him. Plus, it was nice to have a station playing long stretches of music with no commercials or announcements. As he sang along he was surprised at how quickly he came to his next turn. After another twenty minutes, he turned down another road and then another, finally coming to the dreaded long patch of winding dirt roads.

Fortunately for him, the old signs that marked the turnoffs to Bayou Refuge were still in place. In fact, they looked just like he'd remembered. The signs were painted grey with the words "Bayou Refuge" in a fancy font painted dark green. Small brown trees with a few branches—like the kind you'd find in a swamp—were painted along the edges. Charles guessed it was to give the sign a little character. The road itself was a little muddy, and Charles noticed that if he drove more than fifteen miles an hour, rocks and dirt would noisily sling up around his tires. He hated thinking about how dirty his car was going to be after the weekend.

As he drove down the road, he could see through the fog enough to spot the occasional Cajun-style homes, wood houses with porches wrapping around the entire structure. Some even had the old rocking chairs out front, even though no one had probably sat in them for ten years. These old homes had been abandoned after the area began to flood more often as the nearby gulf coastline had worn down over time. The retreat center was really the only place within twenty minutes that was on high enough ground to be safe. The roads had been built up significantly and managed to stay above water when the area flooded. He had driven them a few times after floods, and it was quite an unnerving experience. There had been herds of cattle that would be brought in to graze for parts of the year when it was deemed safe, but they weren't anywhere to be seen today. As he turned onto the next dirt road, as indicated by a sign, large trees covered with Spanish moss hugged the sides of the road. He came to an all-too-familiar part of the road that began to gradually slope up, something not typical on a Cajun road, and he knew he was getting close.

A few minutes later he could see a familiar brown gate next to the entrance of the retreat center. The words "Welcome: Come on In" were on a much larger version of the Bayou Refuge signs, and he drove past, unable to hold back a smile as he recollected happy memories here. He pulled his car up to a large log cabin that functioned as the Bayou Refuge's welcome center as well as housing a small worship center and a few small meeting rooms. To the left of the welcome center was a small, worn-out white wooden house with a green pickup truck parked next to it. A large cypress tree with its top reaching into the fog stood next to the house in an almost picture-perfect way. This was where Claude and Ethel, the groundskeeper and his wife, lived. Judging by the green truck, Charles guessed they had either come back or had worked out some arrangement to stay there despite the camp having been shut down. Claude and Charles always had a nice relationship, so seeing the house and the truck made him look forward to catching up with the man and his wife.

Next to the old white house were a few rustic-looking cabins. They each had five or six rooms for individuals or couples. While they were pretty basic, they had always been well-kept and embodied Southern charm. On the other side of the camp, which was small enough to be seen when one entered the gate, were a few slightly larger cabins. They had open-floor plans and were filled with bunk beds. These were used when the retreat center hosted camps and retreats for larger groups. They'd put the guys in one of them and the girls in another. Behind those cabins and to the left, Charles caught a glimpse of the basketball court and fishing pier. The old cafeteria, walking trail, and seating areas were behind the welcome center.

As he sat in his car and took in the sights, Charles felt like he had climbed into a time machine and gone ten years back in time. Everything looked the same. As much as part of him didn't want to be here, he had to admit there was something great about returning. He parked the car, grabbed his dead cell phone, and headed to the large white doors at the front of the welcome center. He could see lights on and hear some music playing when he suddenly began to feel very weak, almost exhausted, as if he had just run ten miles on the treadmill.

"Oh, man! I think I'm gonna pass out."

He saw an old wooden bench right next to the door and managed to fall onto it and lean against the wooden wall of the cabin. He closed his eyes for a second and heard what sounded like people all around him calmly but urgently talking. He couldn't make out what they were saying. It was almost like he was awake and having a dream at the same time. He shook his head, took a deep breath, removed his glasses, and rubbed his face with his hand. After a moment, the feeling passed, the voices quieted, and the white doors next to him opened.

CHAPTER 4

"Charles, are you okay?" The bald-headed, heavy-set older man wearing blue jeans and a black button-up shirt looked at Charles with concern.

"Hey, Davy," Charles replied as he took a deep breath. He was glad to see his old friend and mentor. "Yeah, I guess I just got weak for a moment. Maybe the stress of the morning is getting to me."

"I bet you skipped breakfast. Come on inside, and I'll get you a cup of coffee and one of Ethel's biscuits. Claude just brought a few over.

Although Charles normally tried to avoid unnecessary carbs, he felt like eating something would probably be a good idea. "Sure, that sounds great. Thanks." Charles slowly got up from the bench and turned to walk toward the door. Davy reached out and put his hand on Charles's shoulder in such a way to catch him if he started to fall. Charles was surprised by the old man's strength. He didn't carry himself like someone who had been battling an illness;

instead, he walked with a confidence and certainty present in much younger men.

The two walked through the white doors and into a welcome area with faded blue carpet and lights that gave a warming orange glow. The wood-paneled walls were covered with pictures from all throughout the retreat center's history. Several chairs and a few couches filled the space, all of which looked clean and cozy, but were products of the '80s and early '90s. Davy motioned for Charles to take a seat on one of the couches, then walked over to a table by a window. The table was filled with the welcome refreshments: coffee, cream and sugar, a plate of biscuits, butter, and assorted jars of jam. Charles watched Davy pour the black coffee into a grey mug with the Bayou Refuge logo on it, then he buttered and put a hefty spoonful of purple jam on a biscuit, set it on a plate, and brought it over to Charles.

"That's homemade blackberry jam by the way," Davy said as he sat down on the couch.

Charles bit into the biscuit and was immediately taken aback by how good it was. The biscuit itself was flaky on the top, soft and crumbly in the middle, and had that perfect flavor of butter and salt. The blackberry jam gave a touch of sweetness that made it irresistible. *This might be the best biscuit I've ever had.*

"She sure knows how to cook them, doesn't she?" Davy said.

"Thanks, Davy." Charles took a long glance at his friend, still impressed by how healthy he looked and how confident he was. It was such a difference from the last time he had seen him. Charles remembered when Davy's wife, Martha, had been leading him around a denominational dinner a while back. He had struggled to remember what was going on and what everyone's name was.

"I'm sorry, but I just have to say that I'm blown away by how much you've recovered. You look better than you've looked in years. I know you have to feel good too."

"Charles, it feels good to be about the Lord's work again. For a while it was like everything was cloudy. I couldn't keep my thoughts straight. I'd often lose track of time. But I have to say these days it's different. I tell you what! Being out in this old place makes me feel more alive than I've ever been. I love being here. I can't stop looking at all these old pictures on the wall. We watched God do some mighty things here. You and I are in more than a few of these pictures. I think I had a little more hair back then. I hope I get to spend a lot more time out here. There's no place like it. Are you feeling better?"

Charles finished chewing and swallowing the bite of biscuit in his mouth, then he washed it down with a sip of coffee. "Yeah, I think I do. What's the game plan for this weekend? What do I need to do to get ready?"

"Well, we aren't set to open on a larger scale. No church groups for the time being. I think Claude is going to do some renovation work on the ball court and maybe get the old ropes course set back up. All that's going on this weekend is a basic Seekers Retreat, just like the old days. I think we've got three people coming in. The first one should come in this evening, and the other two probably tomorrow. You remember the drill. Let them know you're available, and give them space. Make sure they know about the library and when meals are served, then simply be available to talk with them one on one. Listen to them, answer their questions, point them to Jesus and the hope that we have in Him. Tell them how to have a personal relationship with God through Jesus. Charles, I've seen very few young men who could connect with people when they were really seeking quite like you. That's why for this first weekend, I knew I wanted you here."

"Are you going to be here for the weekend too?" Charles asked.

"Oh, I'll be around, in and out some."

"Well what am I supposed to do until this evening? Does Claude need help with anything?"

"I have a feeling a little rest would do you good. Why don't you catch up on some reading and praying, maybe even sneak in a nap. You know my philosophies on naps."

Charles smiles and nodded. "That there's nothing more spiritual than taking a nap. It recognizes that God is in control and that we trust Him to handle the world while we check out of it for a little while."

"That's right," Davy said as a big smile swept across his face.

"Do you know anything about the guests this weekend?"

"Charles, I know they are in desperate need of hearing about the love of God and knowing that He gives second chances."

The two sat for a while longer and made small talk about the fog and how it hadn't lifted yet. They chatted about conferences and meetings from years gone by. About how they had seen God change many lives over the years. They talked about Charles's kids and Davy's grandkids. Charles hadn't been this refreshed by conversation in a long time. After he finished his second biscuit and another cup of coffee, he asked Davy which cabin he was supposed to stay in. Davy slipped him a key to Room 3 in Cabin Two. Charles grabbed the gym bag and extra clothes out of his car and headed toward the cabin. As he made his way there, a sudden of wave of tiredness came over him. All he wanted to do was lie down and close his eyes. Perhaps a nap wasn't such a bad idea.

CHAPTER 5

Room Three was basic, but it was still cozy. It had the same wood-paneled walls as the welcome center, a window looking out into the bayou, and a few paintings of swamp scenes on the walls. One painting was of a sunset scene with some trees, an alligator, and a couple of cranes. The other had a wooden cross standing on a small island in the marsh. Both felt very familiar. In the corner of the room was a desk with an old rotary phone on it. In the center of the room was a full-size bed with a faded red comforter and a couple of matching pillows. Next to the bed was a dresser with a black digital clock on it. Charles noticed that the clock didn't seem to be working even though it was plugged into the wall. Right by the door, in the same manner as most hotel rooms, was a small bathroom. The room was simple, but it was clean and smelled fresh. There was something about it that made him feel at ease, like he was on a much-needed vacation and could just let go of his worries and stress. He closed his eyes and took a deep breath. The smell of the wood and the slight mustiness of the carpet mixed with the same potpourri air freshener that Ethel had used for years transported his mind back to some wonderful memories. He and Deborah had escaped to Bayou Refuge many times over the years before. Ministers could always stay free when there wasn't anything going on at the camp. The rooms not having a television was never a bother. They'd bring cards or board games, stay up late playing them, read books to each other, and have conversations about what the future had in store for them.

Charles was about to sit on the bed when he noticed a note on the desk. When he walked up to it he saw that it was a note from Ethel:

"Charles, it is good to have you back with us this weekend. I understand you were given short notice. We want to do whatever we can to help you. If you need any clothes washed, just set them outside the door in one of the plastic bags in the dresser. I'll pick them up and wash them, dry them, and get them back to you. Praying the Lord uses you. Get some rest and enjoy your time here. Love, Ethel."

That didn't seem like a bad idea, Charles changed into his gym shorts and a T-shirt and placed his dress clothes in a bag he found in the top dresser drawer and set the bag outside the door. He looked down at his phone he had set on the dresser next to his wallet and keys. It was still dead. He suddenly remembered he had an extra charger he kept in his gym bag. He pulled it out, plugged it into an outlet next to the bed, and began to work with the phone. It finally made a ding that indicated it was charging. However, his phone always required a few minutes of charging time before he could use it. He walked over to the rotary phone and picked it up. He listened for the dial tone but heard a strange noise coming through it. It wasn't what he expected it all, and it startled him. It sounded like a pump, something mechanical. He hung up the phone and picked it back up only to hear the same noise. He turned the rotary dial, but it didn't matter. The noise didn't stop. He hung up the phone, slightly aggravated. He felt like he had been cut off from the rest of the world suddenly and had no means to talk to his wife. It was a troubling feeling.

The tiredness that he had temporarily put out of his mind returned to him with a vengeance, and he had no reason to ignore it. So he lay back on the bed, stared through the window out into the foggy bayou, and tried to clear his head. He thought of Connor and Shelby first. He always loved going out to eat, and last week they had all gone to his favorite restaurant, a little hole in the wall. Man, they knew how to fry fish and cook a mean étouffée. Deborah and the kids picked on him because he struggled to eat a meal at a restaurant without spilling something on his shirt. And sure enough, when he went for his first spoonful of étouffée, a few drops fell right off of the spoon and onto his shirt. He bent over a little to try to hide it, but he wasn't quick enough. Shelby had seen it and said, "Mom, he did it again!" He gave them all dirty looks while they laughed, but he cherished moments like those.

He closed his eyes and thought about the last time Deborah and he had been here together on one of those escapes. She was pregnant with Shelby, and it had been a very rough season of ministry. They hadn't been able to get away, just the two of them, since Connor had been born. So on that weekend escape they laughed and celebrated memories from their previous stays while talking about the exciting new opportunities at the church where he was about to start serving. Then they played cards, board games, and Yahtzee while snacking on chocolate chip cookies, all till the wee morning hours. He laughed because he remembered that he barely won any games that night. Deborah had been on a hot streak.

Somewhere in the midst of the memories, sleep found him. It wasn't a dreamless sleep though. He could see the fog while standing out there on the edge of the bayou somewhere, and he could hear voices talking about him and to him, but he couldn't make out what they were saying. He heard the noise that he had heard on the rotary phone. Then he felt the ground shaking underneath him, like it was trying to get away from him. Charles fought to steady himself in the dream, nervous that he was going to fall into the earth or something. Suddenly, everything calmed, and he heard a voice that he recognized. It was Connor's voice, which returned a sense of calm to the dream. Then Charles went from feeling afraid to feeling totally at peace.

"Hey, Dad! I want you to know you're the best dad ever, and I love you. You and I are going to do so many more great things together."

Charles held onto the words like they were an anchor and kept replaying them in his mind. In that moment in his dream he looked out into the fog and could see the sun begin to cut through. He could see that little island in the picture, the one with the cross on it. Then he drifted into a deep, dreamless sleep.

CHAPTER 6

harles awoke from his deep sleep with no way of telling how long he had been out. The fog outside the window looked the same as it had earlier. It still felt like midmorning on a foggy day, no brighter or darker. Something in him longed to see the fog lift. In some ways, it cast not only a shadow over the sun but in his mind as well. He looked at the broken clock next to the bed and at his dead cell phone next to the clock. It hadn't charged at all. Perhaps the spare charger was a dud. He turned his gaze to the window and had to admit that he felt refreshed. The nap had taken away his bone-deep tiredness. He grabbed his glasses and went to the closet where he had placed his other dress pants and shirt. He changed into those and set his shorts on the bed. He wanted to look his best for when guests began to arrive. He knew some pastors liked to dress casual, and he didn't judge them for that. But the men who'd had the greatest impact on Charles had drilled into his head that he ought to look professional amongst people, and he had never been able to let that go.

He went in the small bathroom, washed his face, and wet his short brown hair with just a small amount of water to try and get a stubborn patch of bedhead to lay back down. He made sure his beard looked neat, then grabbed his room key and headed out. He thought now would be a good time to see if Davy or Claude had a cell phone charger. He could also figure out what time it was. The emptiness of the retreat center had been one of its biggest draws to Charles over the years, but in this moment he was really longing to be with another person, anyone. The emptiness was feeling a little creepy.

Charles walked back over to the welcome center but the lights were off. He thought Davy might have left already or ran to town. He saw his car but couldn't see any other vehicle except for Claude's old green truck. But then again, now that he thought about it, he hadn't seen any other vehicle earlier when he came in, so he wasn't sure where Davy had parked. Not wanting to think about how strange that was, he walked over to Claude and Ethel's old white house, then went up the steps to the old creaky porch. The noise made with each step was so loud that it made Charles laugh a little. A burglar would have never been able to get into the house without alerting everyone within twenty yards. The front door had a window at the top, decorated with a thin white curtain. However, the lights were on, and he could see right through the curtain. Claude was sitting in an old recliner in the living room, thumbing through a book. The opening for the kitchen was right behind Claude's chair, and he could see Ethel standing over the stove stirring something. He was surprised they hadn't heard him and come to the door. Charles gave a few solid knocks, right under the wndow, figuring the couple was older and might be a tad hard of hearing. After all, he was a seasoned pastor who had visited many homes. He'd acquired a knack for this sort of thing.

"Claude," Ethel said from behind the stove without looking toward the door.

"I got it," Claude replied from his recliner. "I'm coming."

The old man got up slowly and made his way to the door. Charles could hear the sound of the knob turning, and Claude smiled at him as he opened the door. His friend looked a little older but otherwise pretty good for his age. The man had a skinny frame, which he hid in overalls that were always a size too big. His long-sleeve grey shirt looked stained, worn, and faded.

"Claude, it's great to see you," Charles greeted.

"Come on in, my boy," Claude said with a big smile as he motioned him inside.

"Take your shoes off, please. I just mopped!" Ethel yelled from the kitchen.

"Yes, ma'am," Charles replied with a friendly voice. Claude motioned to his boots on the floor, so Charles slid his dress shoes off, which, in Ethel's defense, already had a bit of mud on them. He set them right next to Claude's work boots.

"Take a seat," Claude said to Charles as he motioned toward another chair in the living room. Charles sat down and noticed that he could smell the pine-scented floor cleaner Ethel must have mopped with and something very appetizing coming from the kitchen.

"That smells amazing. I hope I'm not interrupting lunch."

"Nonsense, dear," Ethel said as she walked into the room. The skinny older lady looked as tough as ever with her perfectly permed white hair and glasses hung around her neck on a chain like an old librarian. Her blue dress managed to look appropriate for working around the house or mingling with church folk at Bayou Refuge. "I thought I was gonna have to send Claude over there and get you for lunch. Can't trust the phones here. I'm glad you came over. If it's all the same to you, we'll just eat lunch here instead of dragging everything over to the café. You know that's what Davy says we're calling the cafeteria now, supposed to be trendy or something."

"Not a problem at all. What's for lunch?"

"Well, I got some red beans and rice on the stove and some cornbread in the oven. Then I've got my crock pot going with some pot roast in it for dinner tonight. Our first guest—Tristan, I believe his name is—should be coming in later today, I'll have it set up for you guys in the café tonight. I'll have some rice, green beans, and pie to go with it. That should take care of y'all."

"That sounds great! Seems like you've got all the bases covered. Thanks for picking up my clothes and washing them for me. This all happened so quickly. I didn't have much time to make sure I had everything I needed."

"Sometimes life happens that way, Charles. You just gotta roll with the unexpected. It all has a way of working itself out the way God intends. We're glad to be here to help you. I know God's going to use you over the next couple of days," Claude said in a reassuring voice.

Claude had always done a great job of encouraging Charles and the other pastors who ministered at the retreat center. In Charles's mind, it seemed like Claude viewed that as part of his ministry. Not just keeping this place running, but helping everyone here feel welcome and ready to get the most out of their time here, whether that was as a seeker, a minister, or some youth or child coming to a camp for the first time.

"I've got those clothes in the dryer. We'll get them folded and back to you. I'll be glad to wash anything else you need. No need to return home with a bunch of dirty clothes," Ethel said. "I like to keep things easy for you. How are Deborah and the kids?"

Charles, still standing by his shoes, began to share his updates on Deborah, Connor, and Shelby. He knew that Claude and Ethel had never been able to have children, and didn't have much extended family either. They seemed to view those who came to Bayou Refuge as the family God wanted them to have. So Charles and many of the other men who came through to minister here made a point to take some time while they were there to get to know the couple and keep them informed of how their families were doing. Claude listened with a smile from his recliner but didn't say much. Ethel kept asking questions, wanting to know as many details as possible. Periodically, she'd move from the doorway to the stove to check on the beans, rice, and cornbread.

Finally, she motioned for the men to come into the kitchen and sit at the small wood table. It seemed to be only made for two, but they pulled an extra chair up to it. Once Ethel set the food on the table and poured everyone a glass of tea, she motioned for Claude to ask for the blessing.

"God, we thank You for this day, for this food before us, for this time to spend with our friend. We ask for Your blessing and touch on Charles as he ministers to these three folks coming this weekend. Use him to help open their hearts and minds to You. God, until we breath our last breath, please find a way for us to be useful to You and Your kingdom. In Jesus' name we pray, amen."

Then the three began to eat. Everything was perfect, just as Charles had expected. He figured Ethel had soaked the beans in salt water overnight, which always enhances the flavor and texture. The smoked sausage in the beans and rice gave just enough of a spicy kick to make the dish pop, and the cornbread had absorbed the butter and went well with the spiciness of the beans.

After a moment of eating, Charles broke the silence. "Do you guys know who the folks coming for the weekend are?"

Claude and Ethel both looked up from their plates. Claude took a swig of tea and then began to speak. "Well, we only know what Davy told us. Based on that, I believe Tristan is coming in this evening. He's a pastor's son who is struggling with whether or not there is a God. Kayla and Martin are coming later. Kayla is a busy mom, very involved with her family, but she has never really stopped to think much about spiritual things. But perhaps she might be open to that sort of thing now. Martin believes in God and considers himself a spiritual man, but Davy says he's missing something."

"Sounds like it should be a pretty interesting weekend," Ethel said.

"Yeah, yeah it does," Charles responded. "Hey, would you guys have a spare cell phone charger I could borrow?"

"No, sorry. We don't do any of that stuff," Claude said.

"You guys don't have cell phones?" Charles asked, a bit perplexed. He felt like that might have come out a bit stronger than he intended.

"No, we don't. Not that you'd get much signal out here anyway," Ethel declared.

Charles thought about that last statement for a moment. As strange as it seemed that at this point in time they didn't have cell phones, he doubted the couple ever went many places and didn't doubt that a signal here would be lacking. "What about the regular phones? What's wrong with them?"

"They come and go as of late," Claude said. "But I've found that if you keep trying them every now and then, you'll get through to someone."

Charles struggled with this because he knew that part of the purpose of being at a place like Bayou Refuge was being able to be cut off from the rest of the world. However, Claude and Ethel should have to have some means of reliable connection with the world. What happens if one of them got sick and needed an ambulance, or if Claude's truck didn't start? Wouldn't they want a phone they knew would work? Yet they seemed to have no concerns or bothers about their lack of ability to communicate consistently with the outside world. Charles felt like drilling them on this for a moment, but he didn't want to be rude. He'd keep his confusion to himself.

"Did Davy leave?" Charles asked.

"Oh, he comes and goes. He'll be back around here later," Claude said.

"Where did he park his vehicle? I didn't see it earlier when I pulled in?"

Claude looked at Charles intently for a moment, then over at Ethel. "Ethel, could I get another glass of this tea? Charles, you gonna go prep and pray in the library after lunch? I know you always liked that place. Ethel's been working hard to get it cleaned up and put together for you," Claude said with a soft smile.

"Yeah, Claude, I think that's a great idea," Charles responded, a bit confused that he had avoided answering the question. "What did you say about Davy's vehicle earlier?" Charles asked, trying to sneakily bring the topic back up.

"Well sometimes I guess he just gets a ride here," Ethel said as she poured Claude a refill of tea. "Would you like another glass, Charles?"

Charles politely declined and smiled. However, as he looked at the couple—Claude finishing up his plate of rice and beans and Ethel putting the pitcher of tea back on the counter—he couldn't shake the feeling that something wasn't right at Bayou Refuge, and it was really starting to bother him.

CHAPTER 7

After lunch, Charles made his way back to his room. He figured he might as well try the phones another time before he headed to the library. As he walked, he continued to replay the lunch conversation in his mind as well as the absurdity of the whole day. He knew God was in control, and he trusted God, but he was human and wanted some indication of what was going on, something to help him get through the next couple of days. Earlier in the day he was convinced that God was leading him to come here. It didn't make full sense, but he was certain of it. Charles firmly believed in the leadership of God through the Holy Spirit, but he hated feeling out of control. In his heart he knew that his desire for control over his day and schedule was the reason for angering Deborah by driving to his meeting despite the fog. It was the reason he ended up hitting the tree branches in the road. His desire to have control was also the reason that right now he was contemplating leaving a note in his room, getting back in his car, and heading home. If the fog was too thick, he'd just drive to the nearest restaurant or gas station and wait it out. At least there he'd be able to borrow someone's phone so he could talk to his wife.

The idea brewed in his mind for a minute as he walked to the cabin. The more he thought about it the more he liked it, even though he felt like he was supposed to stay, and leaving was not what God wanted. Yet he couldn't resist the urge to leave. Why couldn't Davy visit with those coming in for the weekend?

When he got to the front of the cabin where his room was, he looked up, trying to see the sun through the fog. Fog this late in the day, as thick as it was and under these weather conditions, was not common. "God, please let the sun shine through and cut this fog," Charles prayed as he stared up at the sky, hoping something would happen instantly.

He walked into his room and went over to the desk with the black rotary phone. Charles opened the drawer of the desk to look for a pencil and paper to leave a note. Of course there wasn't one; the drawer only contained a brown hardback Bible. Something about it almost felt like it was God calling him out and telling him to stay put. Charles slammed the drawer shut, sat for a moment at the desk, and resolved to stay at Bayou Refuge for the time being. But he would keep his plan to leave as an option. After a moment passed, he picked up the receiver and heard the familiar pumping sound again. He listened to it intently for a moment. It sounded like a machine pumping, and there was an occasional beep. He spoke into it, for no reason at all, just a simple, "Hello! Is anyone there?" He wasn't expecting a response, and wasn't surprised when he didn't get one.

"What in the world is going on?" Charles said in frustration. He had been around phones, like everyone else, for years. He could even remember his grandparents' old rotary phone, but he'd never heard a noise like this, not on a phone anyway. He hit the white buttons that hung up the phone and held them down for several seconds. While they were pressed, he couldn't hear the noise; the line went silent. However, as soon as he released his finger, the machine-like noise, the thumping, and the beeping returned.

Charles took another shot in the dark that he wasn't expecting to work. He held down the button that the phone receiver rested on for several seconds, then released it. Even though he could hear the noise in the receiver, he went ahead and dialed his wife's number. The anticipation was heightened by the fact that it took longer to dial a number on a rotary phone—spin and release, spin and release, spin and release. Not only that, but in his nervousness and desperation, he messed up dialing twice. Finally, after a minute he completed dialing Deborah's number and waited. He heard the same familiar noise and listened for about ten seconds. Just when he was about to put the receiver down, something changed in the noise. The beeping got longer and more intense for a second. Then he thought he heard a voice.

"Deborah, is that you? Can you hear me? Deborah, please answer me."

Charles waited several more seconds, then called out to her again. "Deborah, are you there?"

After a few more panicked moments of hearing only pumping and beeping, Charles called out in desperation, "Is anyone there?"

No one answered. His words seemed to fade into the ether. Charles slammed the receiver down harder than intended, and for a second he thought he might have broken the phone. After picking the receiver back up and looking at it, he was reminded that the quality of this phone was way better than the quality of more modern devices.

"God," Charles prayed, "forgive me for always wanting to be in control. Just let me hear her voice, please. I trust You. I love You. I just want to hear her voice."

Charles took his glasses off and rested his face in his hands. Tears began to fall. He felt stupid, like he shouldn't be feeling this way, but he did. He was glad that no one was there to see him. He wiped his eyes and caught his breath for a moment. As he stood to walk to the bathroom and wipe his face with a towel, he heard an unexpected noise; the old rotary phone rang. It cut through the silence of the room like a hot knife through butter. It felt so unexpected that it startled him, making his heart skip a beat. He listened to it ring a second time but then rapidly picked it up.

"Hello . . . hello?" Charles stuttered into the receiver.

"I don't know how well you can hear me," the familiar voice said on the other end of the line. The voice of his precious wife.

"It's a little staticky, but I can hear you," Charles said through tears. "It's good to hear your voice."

"We're still trying to figure out what's going on, but don't worry, it's okay," Deborah said.

The statement sounded a bit strange, but it made sense that she would be confused if Davy had called her and she had thought he was retired. "Yeah, it caught me off guard too. I'll be home in a couple of days though. I'm really sorry. I feel like I need to be here."

It seemed like she was having trouble getting through. Her words weren't sounding very clear. He could only make out, "We love you . . . kids are . . . church is . . . praying . . ."

"I'm having trouble hearing you, Deborah," Charles said. He heard another patchy mess of words. Nothing that he could make out. "Baby, I'll be home soon. I love you."

"God's got you. Just trust Him, hold onto Him," Deborah said clearly. Then the familiar pumping sound took over the call, and he couldn't hear his wife anymore.

He called out to her several more times, but no response. However, he had to be honest. He was just glad that God had granted him his prayer and he got to hear her voice again. He was pretty sure that God had allowed the call to come through so Charles would know that everything was going to be okay.

CHAPTER 8

Charles headed out of the room and made his way to the old library. It was situated right behind his cabin and next to some pavilions where people could sit, think, pray, and look out into the bayou. Charles made his way into the cabin, which almost looked indiscernible on the outside. If it wasn't for a large sign posted that said "Library," someone would think it was just another cabin.

When he entered the cabin, dim lighting and the smell of old books immediately hit him, not in a bad way though. As an avid reader, this was one of the best smells in the world to Charles. While the retreat center had done very little to keep up with modern works, it had a large trove of classics. Most came from the donations of member churches in their denomination. There were a few wooden chairs and small desks around the edge of the library. The walls of the library were covered with shelves that were probably six feet tall, except where there was a window, which featured a smaller shelf underneath, allowing campers to enjoy the view and the sunshine that normally flooded through. Several rows of shelves filled the middle of the cabin, each six feet tall and built well, made with solid wood by volunteers who had come in to help when the retreat center had been built. Charles remembered all the stories that Davy, Claude, Ethel, and many others who had since passed away had told him about the beginnings of Bayou Refuge, as well as the numerous expansions throughout the years. In the back right corner of the library, there was a little seating area featuring a few cushioned chairs with a coffee table strategically placed between them. This was Charles's favorite spot.

As he walked to the back of the library, he noticed the magazines situated on top of the shorter shelves next to the window. They were the one thing in the library that was kept up to date. Some were filled with daily devotions; others featured topics related to church life, like music ministry, children's ministry, or youth ministry. He saw a few that pertained to certain groups of people. One was geared toward older ladies, another toward urban ministry, and one to teenage girls. He picked up a magazine that had a chipper old lady on it because it looked familiar. When his eyes looked at the date on it, he noticed it was an issue from several years ago. Then he glanced at several of the other magazines and noticed they were all really outdated. He guessed the camp would be renewing those subscriptions, although when he thought about it, he wondered why they had set all of this back out. It was obvious that the library had been cleaned. There were no cobwebs up in the ceilings next to the lights, which for some reason weren't shining bright enough for someone to sit and read with ease. The old, industrial tile on the floor, like what you'd see in a schoolroom, had been swept and mopped. The cushions had been placed just right on the couches. Maybe they were having some issues with the lights.

Charles was a little let down. He had hoped to sit and read in the old cabin and enjoy the view of the bayou if the fog ever lifted. He tried not to think about it too much. Instead, he went and grabbed a Bible and a couple of books by some of his favorite theologians that he had seen in a shelf by the front door. Typically, you were supposed to sign books out if you took them. However, given that he was the only one here, he didn't think Ethel would mind him breaking this rule.

He made his way out of the library and to one of the nearby pavilions. It seemed as good of a place as any to sit and read for a few moments. Charles opened the Bible he had borrowed to the book of Psalms. Even though he knew many of the psalms by heart, he loved reading them and would often read several a day. He found so much peace in them; it helped him think clearly and trust in God no matter what situations he faced.

Not that he knew what time it was or how much time had passed, Charles guessed to have spent twenty minutes or so reading. He started to pray and ask God for help getting his heart and mind ready for the visitors who would be coming to Bayou Refuge shortly. He prayed that God would help him to think less about wanting to be home and to have the focus needed to listen to them and help them. He asked God to give Him the right words to say and to work in their hearts.

Once he was content with his praying, he opened one of the books. It was one he hadn't read in ages but remembered really enjoying it: a collection of sermons from Charles Spurgeon. As he opened to the table of contents, he noticed that the words were smudged and he couldn't really make out what they were saying. Confused, he turned a few pages and noticed the same thing. Then he flipped through the pages with his thumb and realized they were all like that. The only clear wording he could find was the title on the cover. Charles set it down and thought perhaps it had taken water damage at some point, and no one realized it when they donated it.

He opened the next book. It was an old version of Oswald Chamber's *My Utmost for His Highest*, which consisted of daily devotions. Although he had only read through the whole work a time or two, there were a few devotions in it that Charles found particularly meaningful and had read dozens of times. He was encouraged when he opened the book to one of his favorites and reread it, almost able to recite it word for word. The devotional was on faith, and it always managed to encourage him. He flipped to another one several pages later that he always found inspiring. After he read it he began to turn the pages of the book and was taken aback by seeing the familiar sight of pages with smudged, unreadable words. Yet when he turned to a page with a devotion he knew, the words were clear.

"What in the world is going on?" Charles asked no one in particular. He got up from the table and made his way back to the library. Once inside, he began to open books and magazines. The pages were almost all filled with smudged words; the content didn't make sense. In the magazines, some of the advertisements were clear and readable, but not the articles. The books were all almost completely unreadable. He'd occasionally pick up an old favorite and find portions of it readable, but never an entire book. The frustration in him was growing as he grabbed and looked through the books in an increasingly frantic manner. He wasn't putting them back where they belonged but instead dropping them on the floor and grabbing the next one, as if perhaps the answer to what was happening was going to be found in the next book.

After several minutes of this, Charles looked around at the mess he had created. There must have been three of four dozen books sprawled out on the floor; some were open, some had fallen on pages in such a way where the pages were now bent. Charles thought about putting the books back on the shelves, but it felt meaningless. He decided instead to go back to the pavilion and think through things.

"God, what is going on?" he asked as he stood on the edge of the pavilion and looked out onto the bayou. What a day! First the accident on the road, then the call from Davy on his cell phone—which had been dead—then coming out here to Bayou Refuge where some things were great but others just didn't make sense, like the phone. Then there were Claude's comments about Davy's car, and now the library. It all felt like a weird dream.

Was that it? Was this a dream? Charles rationalized how it could explain all the strange happenings. When he thought about it, everything here was as he had remembered it. However, he dismissed the thought because he had never had a dream last this long. Then a thought came to Charles of when this all started, and it made his blood run cold.

CHAPTER 9

Charles played through the morning again in his mind. He had reached down to adjust the radio, turning his eyes for a split second, and then ran over the tree limb. He remembered the car shaking. In the moment it felt violent. It was intense, but there was no damage to the vehicle, and he wasn't injured. It was only then that his phone had worked. That's when things began to happen that didn't make sense. It all started with the tree branch earlier that day.

So what if something else had happened at that moment? Had he died? If he had died, then this went against everything he knew about the Bible and about eternity. Something deep within him almost immediately rejected that. God had responded to him when he asked to hear his wife earlier, and he couldn't deny that he had a sense of peace and calm. Then another thought occurred to him. What if the accident had knocked him out, maybe slung him into oncoming traffic or into the ditch? If he had sustained a serious injury, maybe it wasn't so far-fetched to think that this whole thing really was a dream. That would explain so much, such as the siren he heard but never saw. It would also explain why nothing at the camp had changed. Why Davy had called him in but now wasn't there. Why the phone didn't work right . . .

The noise of the pumping and beeping over the phone sounded a lot like hospital equipment. Somehow, this made everything feel more real, and all of a sudden the weight of the situation hit him. He wasn't dead but in some sort of comatose state! He thought of Deborah, Connor, and Shelby. The thought of them having to live without him broke his heart. Charles had lost his dad when he was in college, and even at the age of twenty-one it was incredibly difficult. There had been a million times since then that he had wanted to call his dad and ask for his advice or go drink a cup of coffee with him and couldn't. He knew how much Deborah not having her father around had hurt her too. He couldn't imagine the struggle she'd have if she lost him. The thought of his kids and wife having to deal with that broke Charles. He took his glasses off and set them on a nearby table and he began to weep, not calmly or quietly but in a very messy way.

After a few minutes he felt a familiar hand on his shoulder. He wiped his eyes and put his glasses back on, then looked up to see Davy. The old man had a soft smile on his face but pain in his eyes. It was a calming presence, one he had seen Davy extend to many people over the years, himself included. Charles nodded his head in thanks and then moved to sit down at a nearby picnic table. Davy sat across from him. Thoughts began to race through his mind again, but not about his family. He was now focused on the nature of this place. What was real, if any of it? And was this really Davy? If so, how could that be? Could he trust what anyone here was saying to him?

"Davy, I have some questions, but I don't know if you can answer them for me."

"I'll do my best, A lot of this I don't understand either. I imagine that you're wondering if any of this real? Are you real? I know how strange that has to sound. It feels real to me, Charles. It feels as real as it felt to sit across from Martha at the dinner table for fifty some odd years. It feels as real as every military skirmish I was in ever felt. It feels as real as it felt that night when Martha told me she was leaving me because I was such an angry man. It feels as real as it felt when I asked Jesus to forgive me of all I said and did in my anger and made Him my Lord and Savior. It feels as real as it did to hold my kids, or preach from behind the pulpit for four decades. I think this is all real in some weird way that I don't fully understand. But if I were in your shoes, I'm not sure if I'd believe any of this either. If it isn't real, would there even be a way to know?" Davy said in an attempt to answer questions he must have figured Charles would have.

Charles felt both comforted and annoyed by Davy's response. Comforted because it was nice to hear someone else recognize the strangeness of the situation; annoyed because it didn't feel like anything had really been answered. "What am I supposed to do with that answer, Davy?"

"Tell me what you think you know," Davy said in a calming, pastoral voice. "Let's work through it together."

"Okay," Charles responded and took a deep breath. "I was traveling to the meeting this morning, and the fog was bad. Deborah told me I shouldn't go, but you know me, I can get pretty stubborn sometimes. It's a two-and-a-half-hour drive. So when I'm about an hour out, maybe more with the fog, I hit something. It was intense. Now that I think about it, way more intense than it should have been for what I hit at the speed I was going. I pulled over to see what it was. A heavy limb and some branches had fallen onto the road from a storm. Then my phone, which had been dead, rang, it was you! You told me to come here. No offense, but someone who can't remember the names of guys he worked with for years, and has to be led around by his wife at get-togethers is now my boss again? How is that right? But you sounded so confident, not confused at all, so I came out this way. The camp is exactly how I remembered it; nothing is different except for the phones and the lighting in the library. When I got here I had a weak spell and could barely stand. I visited with you, ate a bite, then headed to my room where I fell asleep and had the most bizarre dream. I can still hear my son's voice calling out to me. I then got up and ate lunch with Claude and Ethel, who got dodgy when I asked about your vehicle. I messed with the room phone a bit, managed to get a call from my wife, but I could barely hear what she was saying. Then I headed to the library where most of the books were unreadable. That's when I started to question what was really happening. What about you? What's your story?"

"Well, that's a good question. Early on when the dementia hit me, I'd just lose time. I'd find myself sitting in a chair in one room with no memory of how I got there. At first, it didn't happen often, but then it began to happen more regularly. I'd ask for food, and my darling Martha would tell me I'd just eaten. I'd be in the middle of talking with her about something, then the next minute I'd be lying in bed. I figured that was my mind failing, shutting down on me. I have trusted God on my strong days, so I just kept asking Him to help me trust Him on the days when I'm at my weakest, when my health is failing," Davy explained.

"How'd you get here though?" Charles asked.

"Sometimes, instead of suddenly finding myself in another room of the house, I'd find myself back in my office. I'd read pages from familiar books, talk with a few older retired guys, make sure everything there was on the up and up," Davy said calmly. "Then I'd find myself back home again. Sometimes I could swear that I remembered driving home; other times I couldn't. At home, I'd struggle to button a shirt or say a complete sentence, as if my mind was scrambled. But not when I was in the office. Then I remember getting a letter somehow saying that I was being placed in charge of getting Bayou Refuge back in order before my official retirement. Now that I'm talking about it, I can't tell you who wrote it or anything else about it, but I do remember getting the letter. Then I got another one telling me that you'd need to be here this weekend."

"So you're not really better?" Charles asked with confusion in his voice. "Did you lie to me earlier when you said your wife had gotten the medicine changed up?"

"No, not really. Sometimes it's the strangest thing. Some days I'm convinced I'm better, that this is life and I'm doing great. I mean, look at me! I'm better than I've ever been. It seems like these days I spend more time here than I do at home," Davy said, becoming a little more emotional. "You know my story, Charles.

When I got out of the military, I was not a good man. I was angry because of what I'd seen and what . . ." He paused for a moment to collect himself, then continued. "Martha would tell you I was broken and messed up. I wasn't good to her. I wasn't kind to my parents or to my coworkers. I thought alcohol might help me calm down, but it didn't. It only made it worse. I was on the verge of losing everything. Martha left me. I was in that house on my own for a week, and I didn't want to go on. But Martha had left a Bible on the kitchen table, and I began to read it. Let's just say God got my attention. When I finished reading through the Gospel of John, I knew Jesus was calling me to Himself, and I couldn't fight it. He was my only hope. From that point on, I wanted to serve Jesus with all I had because He had saved me. He had kept my family together. My biggest fear after that awakening was becoming useless to God and not being able to help those men of God around me. I watched some old pastors I knew over the years get crippled, weak, and unable to keep their thoughts together to preach a sermon. I know some others who simply got jaded by life and the meanness of people. I prayed God would never let me sit and become useless to Him. Just take me on home when He was done with me on Earth. Charles, I don't know if all of this is God's way of letting me serve Him in some way while my body and mind fade, or if this is all just some imagined world."

The sincerity of Davy caused Charles to pause for a moment before he said anything. They both stared out into the bayou, their minds weighted down by the confusion they shared.

"I've heard of the human brain imagining things as it loses oxygen right before death. I thought maybe this could be that for me. In some ways that would be a lot easier to accept," Charles said.

"I can't tell you that isn't what you are experiencing. It could be," Davy said. "I've always been skeptical of that sort of stuff though."

"So what am I supposed to do?" Charles asked.

"It's a few days," Davy said.

"I don't understand what you mean, Davy," Charles said.

"It's one weekend. I was asked to get you here for one weekend. So if it isn't real, then just go through the motions of it and maybe everything will clear up and make sense when it's done. I mean, if you've been in an accident, maybe by that point they'll know how to bring you back, or they'll let you go. Did you have a living will?"

"Yeah, Deborah and I had talked about something like a bad accident or life support a few times, and we had some paperwork drawn up. She won't leave me like a vegetable," Charles said, oddly enough feeling some peace from the words he had just uttered.

"Then there's the other possibility," Davy said.

"What's that?" Charles asked.

"Well, it's just one weekend, and maybe on this one weekend these three people are in a similar position as you. Maybe this is their last chance to hear about the life-changing love of Jesus Christ. What if your time with them is all that stands between them and eternity?"

Charles didn't know how to respond to that. There really was no way of knowing at this point what was real and what wasn't. He had shared Jesus with people for most of his life. So certainly if this wasn't real, if it was something his mind had put together as he hung near death, then it would make sense that he felt compelled to do this. However, no one really knows fully how the mind works and its connection with the soul. He would certainly never tell others that they would have one more chance right before death to receive Christ, but he wouldn't feel comfortable saying God couldn't work in this way either.

"One weekend," Charles said as he looked at Davy. "I can do that."

CHAPTER 10

The conversation between the two men continued as they began to walk along the bayou.

"Does the fog ever lift?" Charles asked Davy.

"No, I haven't seen it lift yet. It does get a little darker in the evenings, or whenever it decides to. Time doesn't seem to operate the same way here, or our sense of it anyway."

Charles processed that thought for a moment. He knew in some of his more intense dreams that the perception of time was altered. Therefore it didn't seem that odd. Charles looked out onto the water and the most random question came to mind. "Do the fish bite out here?"

Davy began to laugh; it started as a small chuckle but turned into a full-body laugh. "You know, I've been thinking about that for a while now, but I can't work up enough nerve to throw a line in. I might have to ask old Claude about that."

"How are they here, Davy?" Charles asked. "I mean, a husband and a wife out here, and they seem to be here all of the time?"

Davy's grin disappeared, and Charles could tell that he was processing thoughts, trying to figure out how to respond. After several seconds he finally spoke. "I don't know, Charles. They stayed at the camp for several years after it closed, trying to keep it presentable to buyers. There were talks of keeping the house separate from the retreat center so they'd have a place to call their own. I don't think they had much, so this place was the world to them. A few years back I had heard that a niece had helped them get into a nursing facility; both were having pretty serious health issues. Maybe their minds were starting to wear down like mine. I haven't had the courage to ask them. Sometimes I think they know what's going on, but I don't have the heart to bring it up. All I know is that I come and go, but they always seem to be here."

The two continued their walk in silence. Charles followed Davy over to a cypress tree. The old man leaned one of his hands on the tree and then smiled as if he was lost in some memory. "It feels so real. By touch, I can't tell the difference." Charles stopped as well and put a hand on the trunk of the tree, then looked up at the branches and the Spanish moss hanging down. Some branches dropped low enough for him to walk up to and grab; others reached up beyond the fog. "It's like it reaches to the heavens." Davy leaned his head back and tried to look as high up into the tree as he could. "I've heard the old Cajuns talk about these trees my whole life. It's a symbol of endurance. They live where other trees can't. I've heard some say that they're a reminder of eternity because they reach so high it's like they're going to the heavens. Somehow, it feels appropriate here, like they're connected to the roots of where we were and reaching beyond this place. Maybe it's God's way of telling us where we came from matters, but we're also not going to be here forever either. You know all creation testifies."

Charles grinned, appreciating Davy's thoughts. He continued taking in everything around him. He could feel the dampness of the fog, smell the mustiness of the bayou, and remembered how great the food Ethel had cooked tasted. If this was a dream, it was more real than any he had ever had. When Davy began to walk, Charles once again walked alongside him. They were circling around the edge of the retreat center headed toward the entrance of the camp. "Anything you think I should know about being here that you haven't told me yet?" Charles asked.

"Sleep's real strange. I don't sleep much here, but when I do, it's as if I almost pass out, or I'm more tired than I've ever been in my life. The dreams are strange too."

"Mine were earlier," Charles replied.

"Sometimes I just show up somewhere else, like you blink and you're in a different place. It's pretty jarring, but it's okay. I just catch my breath and move on," Davy said. "I'm not sure if that happens to Claude and Ethel though. I've never seen one of them vanish or appear suddenly."

"Like when you showed up at the pavilion?" Charles asked.

"Well, yeah. I mean, I have those moments where I find myself here, and it's like realizing I'm in a dream. I'm here, but I can't remember driving here or anything that happened earlier. Sometimes I'll be here on the bayou, then I'll find myself in the welcome center or at Claude and Ethel's or in my recliner at home. Strangest thing, but I figure it's just the Lord putting me where He wants me. Kind of like old Philip in Acts when God brought him to the Ethiopian."

As they began to come toward the front of the retreat center, they could see Claude walking toward them. The older, skinny man wearing overalls, a grey shirt, and a worn red trucker hat moved slowly toward them. He grinned at the two of them when he got closer.

"What's going on, Claude?" Davy asked.

Claude adjusted his cap and looked off into the fog for a second. "Boy, I sure hope that fog doesn't mess up our first guest's arrival."

"I think they'll get through it okay," Davy replied.

"Well, I sure hope so. This fog just never seems to lift these days, but I suppose it's all in the Lord's hands anyway. Charles, Ethel wanted me to find you and tell you that dinner is ready in the café. Remember, the first guest arrives tonight. He'll meet you there. Davy, if you want a bite there's plenty at the house. Feel free to join us. You know Ethel, my gal, can cook." Claude chuckled a bit with pride in his wife. "It's a phenomenal pot roast."

"Thanks, Claude. I sure am looking forward to it. It's one of my favorites," Charles replied. "Do you know how much longer it'll be until our first guest arrives."

"You know, I can't say that I do, but I can't imagine it would be very long. I just got a feeling he'll be here real soon," Claude replied.

Charles couldn't resist digging a little deeper into Claude's response. "A feeling? What do you mean by that?"

"I don't know. These days I can't explain it. I don't seem to pay much attention to a clock, but I just get a sense when something's gonna happen and it usually does. Maybe it's just a perk of being around for a long time," Claude said with a slight laugh. "What do you think, Davy?"

Charles and Claude both turned to Davy to look for a response, but he wasn't there. Charles tried to think of something to say but came up blank. Claude looked over at him with a smile, but his furrowed brow gave away a hint of frustration. "But you know what? No matter how many times Davy's done that to me, I never get used to it. I don't know how he runs off so quickly or where he goes."

With that comment, Claude headed back to the white house. Charles could see the kitchen light shining through the window. He watched the man make his way back home and could hear the loud creak of the porch as he made his way up the steps and walked into the house. Then he thought about Davy's comments about disappearing to another place and wondered if Davy was still around Bayou Refuge somewhere, or if he had gone back to his home. Charles then made his way to the café to get ready to meet the first guest, praying for God's help and guidance as he walked. Then out of the corner of his eye, something caught his attention moving behind a cypress tree. It was too small to be Davy, but it seemed too big to be an animal. He walked over to the large tree and slowly peered behind it, halfway expecting something to jump out at him. However, nothing was there except the certainty that he had seen something. Despite the desire to continue looking for whatever it was, Charles knew he needed to get to the café.

Chapter 11

Charles sat in the small café, not sure if he had been waiting for an hour or ten minutes. The building had probably seven or eight tables that could each seat five or six people. There was a large wooden foldout table with metal legs set up against the wall where the crockpot with the pot roast was sitting as well as some mashed potatoes, green beans, a plate of homemade rolls, a pie, a pitcher of tea, and a pitcher of water. Some blue plates were situated at the end of it as well as cups and silverware. On the walls surrounding the café were several pictures of nature scenes with Bible verses on them. One was the sun setting behind some mountains; another showed a herd of wild horses running. There was a small wooden counter with an old cash register for when concessions were sold on certain weekends. Charles could make out boxes of various candy bars on a shelf behind it. The lighting was perfect; it was bright enough to make everything easy to see but just dim enough to make it a bit more comfortable to have a serious conversation. The wooden chairs with thin, orange cushions were surprisingly comfortable.

As he sat back and waited, part of him thought about going ahead and fixing a plate of food. Charles figured that since this may not even be real, surely there wouldn't be any harm in eating something before his guest arrived. However, he could hear the voice of his mother in his head. She had always been a stickler for etiquette. So he waited . . . and waited . . . and waited.

Finally, after what felt like an eternity, perhaps because like everyone else, he had grown accustomed to having his phone to fiddle with while he waited and wasn't used to waiting while doing nothing, the door began to open. He turned, expecting to see his first guest, but was surprised to see Ethel coming through the door with a butter dish. He smiled and tried to hide his disappointment.

"I'm so sorry! I forgot the butter dish," Ethel said. "I don't know what's wrong with me today."

"If that's the worst thing you do today, you'll be in good shape," Charles replied, trying to reassure her. He watched her as she set it down on the table next to the rolls. Ethel then looked over everything, opening a few lids, trying to make sure everything was up to her high standards.

"I think everything is set."

"It looks wonderful. I'm sure it is going to be great."

"Well, I sure hope so. You have a wonderful night," Ethel said as she walked toward the door.

"You too."

But when Ethel neared the door, she stopped and placed her hand on a chair and leaned on it. She suddenly looked very confused. Her legs wobbled a little, like she was having trouble standing. Charles was both confused and concerned at the same time. Then he remembered the spell he'd had earlier in the day. Perhaps this was something similar.

"Ethel, are you okay?" Charles asked as he got up and walked over to her.

She was slow to respond. She just stared at the floor and turned her head a little. "I . . . uh . . ." was all she managed to get out.

"Ethel, talk to me," Charles said with a bit more firmness in his voice. "What's going on?"

"Uh, I don't . . . What's happening?" Ethel looked up at Charles, who pulled out another chair and motioned for her sit down when he felt her hand grab his arm. It was weak, and it surprised him to see her this way. He wanted to help but had no idea of what to do.

"Sit down, Ethel." Charles calmly guided her to the seat. She sat down and finally looked him in the eyes. There seemed to be some sort of calm and ease about her now. Like perhaps whatever had gone on had passed. This was encouraging because if this was real, he had no idea of what to do to help her. The way this world functioned was different. He figured there would be no chance of getting a 911 call out.

He walked over to the table, poured a glass of water, and brought it over to Ethel. She gave him a look of thanks and then slowly took a sip, her hands shaking a little as she did. In this moment Charles didn't see the Ethel he had known for years—a strong, independent woman who could do anything. Instead, he saw a feeble elderly woman.

"I'm so sorry," Ethel said to Charles, genuinely embarrassed. "I don't know what that was about?"

"Has that ever happened before?"

Ethel thought for a moment and took another sip of water. She set the glass down on the table and tilted her head to the side. "No I don't believe it has. I just felt weak, like I could barely stand, like I was about to fall asleep standing up. My legs feel very strange. I feel better now though. I must have overdone it when I was cleaning the library this afternoon. I think some animal or something must have gotten in there. It was a mess."

Charles put his head down and thought about whether he should confess to making the mess or not. But his hesitation was short-lived. "I might have had something to do with that. I'm so sorry."

"Hmm, this is a strange day," Ethel replied, looking at him first with confusion, then with compassion. "Well, do be more careful next time, please. I don't think we'll get any more books out here."

"Yes, ma'am," Charles said with a hint of embarrassment in his voice.

"It's all forgiven. Life's too short to hold on to stuff."

"Let me walk you back home to make sure you get back okay."

"Well, I don't think it would be wise to turn you down. I'd be glad for the company. I just don't want you to be late for your dinner guest."

"I think it'll be okay."

He helped Ethel get up out of the chair, and the two made their way to the door. She linked her arm through his. When they came to the small step by the door, Charles urged her to be careful. She nodded, and the two walked back toward her home. Even though the fog had not lifted, it was clearly nighttime. There were a few lights hung on the edge of some cabins that made the path visible. Plus, Charles could see the light of a lamp shining through the living room window of Ethel and Claude's house.

Although Ethel had said she was glad for the company, there was little chatter on the way back. Charles could see in Ethel's face that she was trying to figure something out. Perhaps she, too, was wondering what was really happening. As they got closer to the house, Charles could see Claude standing on the front porch. When Claude saw that Charles was walking with Ethel in a way that indicated she needed help, the old man jogged down the steps toward them.

"Ethel, are you okay?" Claude asked when he reached her. He looked her up and down, making sure everything was all right.

"Oh, I'm fine. Just had a weak spell, that's all."

"Well, maybe we ought to . . ." Claude began, then stopped himself. Charles assumed he was thinking about calling 911 or going to the hospital. "Well, never mind. We'll just keep a good eye on you tonight."

"I'm grateful that Charles here was able to help make sure I got back home okay."

"Thank you, son," Claude said.

"Do you need me to do anything?" Charles asked.

Claude thought for a few seconds as he turned toward his home. "No, I don't suppose so." With a hint of sadness in his voice, he added, "Maybe say a prayer for her."

Charles walked over to Claude and Ethel and put his hand on both of their shoulders, then prayed over the couple, as he had many times as a minister with hundreds of people. He asked for God's healing touch, His strengthening over the couple, and His hand over the evening. Once he said amen, the couple said goodnight and he made his way back to the café.

When he opened the café door, he was a bit startled to see a man with dirty-blonde hair who looked to be in his late 20s or early 30s. He was sitting at a table with a plate of food in front of him and a fork in his mouth. He was wearing an unzipped brown leather jacket with an expensive-looking red T-shirt underneath. He looked like he hadn't shaved in a day or two. Charles looked down to see the man's expensive blue jeans shaking a little as his brown boots tapped the floor.

"Good evening. And you are . . . ?" Charles asked.

"I'm Tristan. What's up?" His voice held little emotion.

CHAPTER 12

Perhaps it was the casual tone in his voice, or that he just wasn't expecting to see someone in the café when he opened the door, but Charles was definitely caught off guard. Where had Tristan been? Had he just appeared here instead of driving? Then he looked at the full plate of food Tristan was enjoying and thought that perhaps he should have gone on and fixed a plate and eaten earlier when he had been tempted because it seemed clear that his first guest was not a stickler for etiquette. Charles had a lot of questions, but he didn't want to bombard his guest.

He walked over to the table where Tristan was seated and extended his hand. Tristan put down his fork, wiped his hand on his pants leg, and extended it for Charles to shake. "I'm Charles."

"Props to whoever cooked this meal. It's top-notch. I like this whole rustic thing you've got going on here."

"Thanks. Mind if I join you?"

"Be my guest," Tristan responded as he watched Charles go over to the table with the food and fix a plate. Since he didn't even know how real any of this was, Charles once again gave little concern for his diet and piled his plate high, cut a large piece of pie, and poured himself a large glass of sweet tea.

Charles walked over to the table and set his food down across from Tristan, sat down, and looked at his guest before taking a large sip of tea. Tristan gave a quick smile as he chewed his food. Charles could detect just a hint of unease in Tristan, which was to be expected. "Where are you from?" Charles asked before he took a large bite of pot roast."

"Little place in East Texas," Tristan said. "Been in New Orleans the last several years though."

"Work bring you out there?" Charles said as he took another bite.

Tristan set his fork down on his nearly empty plate and finished chewing for a few seconds before he spoke. "No, not really. I just thought I had to get out. So first chance I had to go somewhere else—somewhere different— I took it."

"How's that worked out for you?" Charles asked.

"I don't know," Tristan responded with some hesitation. "Probably not like I thought it would. But I guess nothing ever really lives up to our expectations."

Charles took his last bite of pot roast, then he took his roll and wiped up the juice from the meat before finishing the roll. He pushed the larger plate to the side and moved the plate with his pie in front of him. He was struggling a bit, trying to figure out the best way to get Tristan to open up to him. He'd had tons of these conversations with people over the years, but the uncertainty of everything around him and the feeling of having little control over anything going on around him was making him second-guess himself. After a several seconds, he blurted out the first question that came to mind. "What kind of work did you get into out there in New Orleans?"

"A little bit of everything. I've waited tables, bartended, made deliveries, worked as a bouncer for a little while, you name it," Tristan replied. I just tried to find stuff that let me experience life to the fullest, you know."

"I think I can respect that," Charles said, thinking maybe a door to deeper conversation may have opened. "Everyone is kind of searching for meaning and purpose."

A sly grin came on Tristan's face, one that made Charles wonder what was going through his mind. After a few moments, Tristan revealed his thoughts. "This is where you try to tell me about Jesus and how I need a relationship with Him? You know I've heard that spiel before. I don't think I'm buying."

Charles appreciated Tristan's openness and realized the conversation might be more challenging than he had hoped. Perhaps Tristan wasn't as ready to talk about spiritual things as had been implied in Claude's comments earlier. "Well, what brings you out here? There's got to be some struggle in your mind happening, or you must be looking for something."

"I don't know. I grew up around God, football, guns, and country music. It all seemed so fake. People coming through the church doors on Sunday, listening to the preacher talk about how sinful the world was and how mad God was at everyone while they acted like they had it all together and were the exceptions to the rule, all high and mighty. But during the week they talked bad about their neighbors, hid liquor in their cabinets, and were sleeping with their neighbor's wife. Just hard to take God seriously in that setting," Tristan said.

"I can appreciate that," Charles replied. "Was it that way in your family too?"

"You know, for the longest time I didn't think so. I thought my mom and dad really believed the stuff. I would have told you that I was one of the lucky kids who had a family that practiced what they preached. And you know what? My dad did preach. He was the preacher, and man he could preach. He could talk about God's anger, the sins of the world, and how we had to live right that he certainly had me convinced for a long time."

Charles could see Tristan become angry, and his face turned a little red. He realized that this was a hard topic for him. So as Tristan sat there, unable to finish the thought, Charles took a bite of pie and sat in the awkward silence. "You don't have to talk about this if you don't want to."

Tristan shook his head. "No, that's just it. No one ever really talks about anything, myself included. Growing up, no one had enough guts to put it all in the open and recognize everything for how messed up it really was. My dad started sleeping with the church secretary, and everyone in the church knew about it, even my mom. But no one would dare talk about it. I mean, they'd whisper to each other in the parking lot, but no one would call him out. Here's a man who was supposed to tell everyone else 'the truth' and 'guide them.' A man who said, 'Fear the righteous anger of the Lord! Don't tempt the Lord by hiding sins.' And what was he doing? You know, my mom tried to act like everything was okay. She wouldn't talk about it either. Just kept it all bottled up and got hooked on whatever pills the doctor gave her to help with the depression. This went on for months until the secretary's husband finally told her this had to stop. When the secretary told my dad it was over, he and the deacons had her fired, and life was supposed to go on like nothing had ever happened. That's when I decided I was done with church, done with God. I was going to do my own thing. As soon as I graduated from high school, I packed my bags up and headed to New Orleans in the middle of the night without ever looking back."

Charles was thankful Tristan's candidness, even though it would make some people uncomfortable. As a pastor who sought to walk with God, although he was far from perfect, he recognized that many people, dare he say most people, knew a version of Christianity—something that was more about a show, or a set of rules and expectations than it was about actually knowing God through a relationship with Jesus Christ. Words like *surrender* and *repentance* were replaced with a sort of self-righteous legalism that gave the person a free pass to sin while also being able to look down on the sins of others. Many people fell into the trap of making Christianity a series of political beliefs that focused on some scriptural obligations while rejecting others. The conversation Charles was having with Tristan was the type of conversation he lived for, opportunities to help someone consider the difference between cultural Christianity and genuinely knowing and walking with God. Charles finally felt like he was getting comfortable in this situation.

Regardless of how strange the rest of Charles's day had been, this moment felt real. In fact, to Charles, there seemed to be nothing strange or off-putting here except for the fact that Tristan seemed to just appear in the room and was eating a meal when Charles entered with no apparent concern for where he was or what was happening. He finished off the last of his pie as he watched Tristan get himself a piece and then sit back down.

"I thank I'm going to get some of that coffee?" Charles said, turning his head to the old concession stand where the coffee, sugar and creamer had been placed. "Want some?" Charles offered after a few moments, trying to busy himself after the awkward silence that followed Tristan's personal story.

"Yeah, thanks," Tristan said. "Grab a few of those cream and sugar packets if you can."

"Sure thing." Charles got up and walked to the counter, then began to pour two cups of coffee. "So what happened when you got to New Orleans?"

Tristan didn't say anything, and his silence made Charles turn and look back toward the table where Tristan was holding his fork and giving Charles a strange look.

"You okay?"

"Yeah, just a little surprised that you're still listening to me and not trying to offer some easy answer or explain away what happened to me."

"Well, if you're ever going to listen to me, I've got to spend some time listening to you. Plus, I try not to offer easy answers because I hate it when people offer them to me."

"I can appreciate that. I'll be really honest then, if you're gonna listen," Tristen said.

"Go ahead," Charles replied as he set Tristan's coffee in front of him and took a seat, sipping his black coffee.

"I made a decision when I went to New Orleans that I was going to go all out. Anything I felt I wanted to do I was going to find a way to do. I wasn't going to deny myself anything. You know, my whole life I had been told that religion was about a set of rules, that somehow God's forgiveness was free but I had to keep these rules too. I figured if the people teaching me this stuff didn't take it seriously, why should I?" Tristan took a bite of his pie and a sip of coffee, then pushed the plate away from him. "Dad hated New Orleans, always talked about how horrible and godless it was. He said there was nothing but pagans there. I'll be honest. I wanted to get as far away as I could from that man, so I figured New Orleans would be the last place he'd ever come to look for me. I'd just hide out amongst the pagans. First week I was there, I got a job bussing tables at a restaurant. One of the guys at the restaurant let me crash on his couch for a couple of months til I had enough cash to go in with a few other folks and get an apartment. The place was a dump, but it was home. Then I started really getting into the

New Orleans party scene. Alcohol, drugs, sex—whatever. I jumped into all of it. I got pretty good at balancing it with my work life too. Heck, before I knew it, they had promoted me to waiter, then bartender. Life was good."

"How'd that work out?" Charles asked.

"I wasn't making a ton of money, but it was plenty for me—for a while anyway," Tristan replied. "But I started getting into some harder stuff, and I was tired of living in a dump. So when one of the guys I worked with told me he was leaving to go be a bouncer at a club and there was another opening if I was interested, I went and did that for a while, made some deliveries for a courier service during the day. The money was good, but I got tired of people threatening to beat me up. So I went back to waiting tables and started doing some less-than-legal things to earn money."

Tristan didn't say anything for several seconds, then Charles pushed his empty plate back a little and finished his cup of coffee, and the two sat once again in awkward silence. Charles had learned a long time ago in counseling training to not be afraid of silence.

"I was good at it too," Tristan said. "I didn't just sell drugs, but I figured out how to move large quantities of drugs and get them to guys in the area who wanted to sell them. I don't know why, but I just had a knack for figuring out the ways we could get caught and working around them. Made enough money to support my own habit. Managed to buy a house, a nice car, and live a pretty easy life."

"What changed?" Charles asked.

"I heard that one of the ladies at the restaurant where I started at had a fifteen-year-old son who died of a drug overdose," Tristan said while looking at the table. "I mean, that stuff happens, but I began to wonder if I had played a role in it. Was it something I had helped move? Had I helped kill this kid?"

"Man," Charles said, "that's rough."

"You know, for years I lived thinking I was better than everyone back home. That I wasn't a hypocrite playing some stupid game. That I was open about what I was doing and wanted to do and had nothing to hide. I was going to live a life that was full of what I wanted to do, and I wasn't going to be a hypocrite. Yet here I was, working a job where I had to hide what I was doing from the public, telling myself it didn't really hurt anyone. Adults can do what adults want, all while knowing that there was no way to guarantee that it was staying in the hands of adults. Telling myself that no one was paying a price for what I was doing. Yet at the end of the day, I was no better than my dad. I spent years trying to separate myself from him, and in the end I had become just like him."

"So what did you do?" Charles asked.

"I overdosed," Tristan replied. "I didn't care if I died or wound up in the hospital. I was just going to take as much as I felt like. Last thing I remember was getting sick, sweating, and passing out. Then I woke up here."

CHAPTER 13

"So where do you think *here* is?" Charles asked, leaning in a bit closer, eager to hear Tristan's thoughts.

Tristan looked around the room for a moment, then stared at Charles as if trying to solve the mystery before responding. He didn't look angry or confused, only puzzled, like he had just heard a riddle and was trying to solve it. "I don't know. I've done a lot of drugs over the years and have had some strange dreams and trips. I figured after all I took, this must be my brain reacting to the chemicals I put into my body. Although I have to say, you asking me this is tripping me out a little."

Tristan's nervousness caused Charles to once again think about how he viewed his own experience here. It all felt so real. Was there any way Charles had imagined or dreamed that Tristan was there? Charles had to admit that this whole experience was making him quite uncomfortable as well. He had always assumed that people who were unconscious or comatose were in a sleep-like state where nothing was perceived. But he had heard of people having near-death experiences where they claimed to see things or understand things that were a bit beyond normal human understanding. If God had called Charles to share the gospel with others in his regular day-to-day life, surely he could share in this state too. Perhaps God was testing Charles to see if He'd be obedient, to extend one last invitation to those who were somehow on the edge of life and death.

"You said you were questioning things after your coworker's child died. Did you ever think that maybe your understanding of God is wrong?"

"I don't know how to answer that," Tristan said in a tone that conveyed confusion and frustration. "If you would have asked me a year ago if I had any doubts, I don't think I would have had any, or at least any big enough that I'd feel like I need to admit to them. But now, I don't know. Growing up I heard of a God who supposedly loved me but, who seemed to be ready to strike me dead if I disobeyed Him. I always felt like God was going to be disappointed in me no matter what I did or how hard I tried. For a long time it frightened me, made me feel guilty about everything I did—whether it was watching something on TV, listening to music that wasn't considered Christian. I was even paranoid about the thoughts that sprung up in my head. Then when my dad did what he did, it made me think that the whole thing was a sham. Now I can say that over the years I heard some talk of a loving God who changed lives and filled people with peace and joy, but I don't know how much of that I ever saw it back in the church my dad pastored."

"You've never seen that love lived out? Not by anyone?" Charles asked, hoping to get Tristan to reevaluate his answer.

"I mean, I guess there were like a few old people in the church I grew up who seemed to really believe that God had sent Jesus to die for them and had really given their life to God. They studied the Bible, tried to encourage others, and never seemed to fall into the gossip and the judging of other people. However, they definitely weren't the norm," Tristan said. He sat back in his chair and his brow furled a little.

"You look like you're remembering something," Charles said.

"Yeah, there's this guy, old Black preacher, Reverend Jones, who'd walk through downtown New Orleans and try to visit with anyone who would talk to him." Tristan chuckled and smiled a little. "Reverend always had a smile on his face, and when he'd say your name he would laugh and lean in for a handshake. And let me tell you, he had a grip. Sometimes he'd pull you in for a big old hug. He came into the restaurant I worked at for a while, then I'd see him walking the streets down there. He'd always want to talk. Often it would start off about football, a new restaurant that opened, or the weather. However, usually it wound up deeper than I really wanted to go. But also there was something comforting in it, like maybe I was getting closer to understanding something that eluded me," Tristan said, looking down at the table, lost in thoughts of those old conversations.

"What did you guys talk about during the deeper conversations?" Charles asked as he leaned back in his chair after several seconds had passed.

"Life, family, church, Jesus—anything really," Tristan replied. "It wasn't just me; he tried to talk to everyone. So I just got a sense that even though I didn't agree with his idea of a loving God, or if there even was one, I was curious that God would want anything to do with me. I figured He must be a good guy and worth knowing. The reverend would ask me questions about my family, such as if I'd let God help me and if I could forgive my dad. I'd tell him that there was no way I'd ever forgive my dad. I experienced such hypocrisy and pain from a guy who made a living telling other people not to do the kinds of things he did. Even if I could forgive him, why would I want to? He'd ask me about really receiving Christ, letting Christ forgive me and giving Him my life. That was always followed by telling me that then I'd be able to watch God do things in my life that I couldn't even imagine. Those conversations were usually pretty short. The seriousness would stop when I got too uncomfortable, then we'd pick on each other and go back to talking about the Saints or the weather. But he was different from my dad; it felt like there was something real there. Something I'm not sure my dad ever had. I had never really seen that kind of hope and joy lived out by him."

"Do you think your dad didn't know Christ? Or maybe it doesn't matter because there's no Christ to know?" Charles asked while looking Tristan in the eyes.

"That's straight to the point. I can appreciate that," Tristan said with a bit of a smile. "I questioned all of it. Thought my life would be so much better without any kind of faith. Like I'd not only hold it together, but I'd be way better off. Now look, I know some folks may be able to hold it together all on their own, or at least it looks like they can. But me? I don't want to go back to what I had. Although maybe going back isn't even an option. But there's a part of me that knows the facts, the arguments on why there's a higher power and the absurdity of life coming from nothing and why the Bible makes a lot of sense. But it's just hard to accept it, you know?"

"Why?"

"Because I'd bet so much on it not being true. I tried so hard to prove I was better than my dad and better than those people, and I'm not. I'd really rather just push through a little longer and just die in my pride. I know that makes no sense. I know that if the Bible is real, then that means there's a hell, and I shouldn't be okay with going there. But come on! God kind of set me up for this. I'm supposed to love God and trust him after what He's allowed me to go through? Who does He think he is? He could have stopped this crap from ever happening," Tristan said with anger and sadness in his voice. After he spoke, a tear fell from his left eye.

"Tristan, I don't know if this place we are in is real, if you're real, or if I'm dreaming this whole thing in a hospital bed because I'm not getting enough oxygen to my brain. If it is real, I really don't know what happens when we finish this conversation and you walk out of that door. I don't know if you get to wake up, or if you go into eternity. This could be the last conversation on this side of life that you ever get. I don't think it's fair that you had to go through what you went through growing up. I think that's really messed up. Sometimes people get the wrong idea about God, one that isn't really rooted in His Word, which reveals to us the rich love He has for us. These people don't understand how to really know or love God, so they can't help others know or understand God. Maybe your dad just got the wrong idea of who God is because it was handed down to him incorrectly. I'm sorry he didn't do better. I'm sorry he hurt you. The people who should have been there for you weren't. But He did send you Reverend Jones. He's sent me. God is still reaching out to you. God in His mercy is possibly giving you another opportunity to find His grace and receive His love. Like the thief on the cross, you've got a chance, but it probably isn't a very long one. Will you ask Him to help you let go of that hurt and anger, or are you going to die with it?"

"Is this the alter call?" Tristan said with a smirk. "I've heard this sermon before, but this has to be the first time I'm hearing it where the preacher asks, 'If that door leads to eternity . . .' and it might really be true."

Tristan and Charles both laughed a little. The tension eased for a few seconds as Charles watched Tristan think intensely about what he was going to do. Tristan looked down at the table for a moment, then looked back up at Charles. He scooted the chair back and was about to stand, and Charles was convinced he was going to walk out of the café door, holding onto his anger and bitterness, rejecting God. However, instead of standing Tristan got on his knees as tears began to fall from his eyes. Part of Charles couldn't believe what he was seeing. God had done a work in Tristan's heart.

With desperation in his voice, Tristan cried out, "God, I am a horrible, broken man. I have sinned. I have rejected You. I have pursued things that go against You. In trying to prove my father wrong, I have revealed that I am just as messed up as him. God, I need Your forgiveness through Jesus. I turn from my sins. I give you my life. Whether I get to wake up in my apartment or I wake up in eternity, it's Your life now. Take it. God, take away my anger toward my father and the church where I grew up. Forgive them, and help me to forgive them too. Please be merciful to those who have been hurt by my bad choices. I love You, and I need You. Please, save me. Take my life . . ."

Charles had closed his eyes as he listened to Tristan pray and felt a sense of calm and peace unlike any that he had ever felt before. What he had just heard was one of the most powerful prayers he had ever heard someone pray, and he could tell that it was filled with sincerity. Charles opened his eyes to congratulate his guest on his decision to give his life to Christ, then realized he was now alone in the room.

Tristan was gone.

CHAPTER 14

Charles looked all around the room and then walked over to the door and opened it. He scanned the fog-filled darkness, intently hoping to catch some glimpse of Tristan.

"Tristan!" Charles called out, but there was no response. He came back into the room and thought for a moment about the conversation he'd just had. It seemed that God had softened Tristan's heart. He had become open to the idea of faith in Christ despite all that had happened in his life. God's mercy never ceased to amaze Charles. Whether this was real or not, it was a great reminder of the goodness of God.

Then Charles's mind turned to what happened to Tristan and where had he gone. Had he woken up back in his house or in a hospital room somewhere? Maybe he died and had entered into eternity. Or was this all just something happening in Charles's mind? Even though his disappearance shouldn't have surprised Charles, it did. He felt like Jim Gordan when Batman disappeared mid-conversation. He guessed that whatever had happened to

Tristan wasn't his concern now. He muttered a quick prayer for the young man and then looked around the empty room.

His mind began to drift back to his own predicament. He craved his own bed next to his wife, knowing that his kids were fast asleep in their rooms. He wanted to wake up to coffee from his own coffee pot and to sit in his recliner while he drank it and watch the squirrels playing in the magnolia tree. The thought of home put a smile on his face. However, it didn't take long for the realization that he might never return there to come back to his thoughts. Would he suddenly just disappear like Tristan, either into eternity or to his home? This all had to end at some point, right?

Charles tried to clear his mind a bit by picking up the dishes at the table and setting them next to the food-serving dishes Ethel had set out. Even though this wasn't necessary work, he felt obligated to pick up after himself a bit. Ethel had seemed too weak earlier to do much, and her episode had startled him. If this was some sort of altered, in-between state for the soul, then when the body and mind were fading, could it be that Ethel's body was giving out and was about to die? The whole thing made his mind ache a little bit.

He forced himself to focus on the work at hand and thought about bringing the leftovers over to Ethel and Claude's house, but didn't know if they'd still be awake. When he stepped outside and looked over toward the white house, he noticed there were no lights on. So he figured he might as well head over to his cabin and try to get a little rest. Mostly because he didn't know what else to do in order to pass the time.

The fog was really thick, and the lights that hung on poles and the edges of cabins struggled to cut through the fog. He could only see a few steps ahead of him, but he trusted that God would get him to his room if he walked in the general direction. Slowly, one step at a time, he made his way back. Once he got back to Cabin Two, the soft orange lights in the hallway led him to his room.

The lamps in his room were on: one next to the bed and one next to the phone. Looking at the black rotary phone made him nervous. Something about it was both hopeful and petrifying. The sounds of the machines were unnerving and made him feel like death was coming for him. But the possibility of contact with the outside world, with his wife and children, was comforting and felt like receiving a priceless gift. Charles sat on the edge of the bed and stared at the phone for a few moments. All he could think about was picking it up, but he couldn't find the nerve to do it. He just knew that the only thing he'd hear would be the noise of the machines: pumping and beeping.

He felt like sleeping. A tiredness had come over him, not like before, but more like being worn out after a long day. He changed into his gym shorts, crawled into the bed, and turned off the lamp by the bed but left on the one by the phone. His eyes turned to the paintings on the wall. The painting of the swamp at sunset was hypnotic; he got lost in it for a few minutes. Then he gazed at the image of the island with the cross on it. Thoughts of the dream he'd had earlier that day came to mind.

Charles didn't remember closing his eyes, but when he opened them he was by the pavilion. It was daytime again, and the fog had lifted. He could feel the warmness of the sun on his face.

A cool breeze made the Spanish moss in the trees dance. He smiled. There was something about being able to see into the distance, being able to hear birds chirping and the occasional splashing of water as fish jumped that made him feel normal again, like he was back in his regular life. He knew he was dreaming but he didn't care.

As he looked around he saw someone else seated at a table. It was Shelby, his daughter. She was wearing her favorite purple T-shirt, and her long brown hair was pulled in a ponytail. She was reading a book. Charles walked over to where she sat. Shelby looked up from her book and smiled at him.

"Hey, Daddy."

"Hey, baby girl," Charles responded. *Baby girl* was a nickname he had called her by since she was born. She loved it when he called her that. "It's so good to see you."

"We love you so much," Shelby said. He could hear the sadness in her voice. "I hope you aren't hurting too much."

"Not at all. I'm okay."

"Mom says we need to make sure you aren't suffering. She says that's the important thing. I understand. I just don't want to let you go. I know she doesn't either. She's trying really hard to hang on. We all are."

Charles began to wonder, based on Shelby's words, if he was hearing what she was saying from the hospital room. Maybe this wasn't a dream. Perhaps she was really communicating with him. If that were the case, then it didn't do much good to talk to her, but he'd try anyway. It didn't feel right not to. "I'm not suffering. I promise. I can't say that I fully understand what's happening to me, but I'm okay. I just miss you guys a lot."

"Connor's having a hard time. He's trying to act tough, but he's crying a lot when he thinks no one sees him. It hurts a lot, but I'm trying to remember what you always told us. God walks with us through the good and the bad, so I know He's with me. There are so many people praying for you."

Tears began to roll down Charles's face. The thought of leaving his two children behind was painful. Charles felt his anxiety escalate; his lack of control over anything was overwhelming. So much of his time went into planning his day-to-day activities for the church and for his family, working to balance everything, and overall it seemed to work. Charles felt like he'd had a level of control over life. However, facing the reality that he was powerless here and totally dependent upon the Lord was hard for him to accept. It was embarrassing that someone who preached trusting and walking with the Lord so much would feel so out of place in a situation where he was having to do just that. Then he felt a squeeze on his hand and suddenly became aware of the fact that Shelby was holding his hand. It was such a wonderful feeling, and it freed him from his tormenting thoughts. He could feel her touch; it really seemed like her. It would make sense that she'd be holding his hand. Charles just looked at her, proud of who she had become and comforted by her presence. She was growing into such a wonderful young woman who was focused on seeking God and honoring Him.

No more words were exchanged between the two of them. What she had said was probably hard enough for her to say, and he didn't want her to feel obligated to say anything else. Being there with him in this moment meant so much. He had always heard that people in the hospital valued having someone there to talk to them and hold their hands even if the patient was unconscious. This made more sense to Charles now than it ever had before.

After a few moments, the sound of an alarm going off shook the world of the dream apart, and Charles opened his eyes to find himself back in bed in the cabin. A little sunlight was pouring in through the fog and lighting the room. The noise sounded again, and Charles realized that the phone in his room was ringing.

CHAPTER 15

His whole body tensed. He wanted to lie there and think about the encounter with his daughter. However, he knew he had to answer the phone. Yet the thought of what he might hear also scared him. He wanted it to be Deborah so badly, to hear her say he was getting better, but part of him felt like that was highly unlikely. He forced himself to walk over to the phone and pick up the receiver. Immediately, his ears could make out the familiar sound of a machine making a pumping noise along with an occasional beep. At first, that's all he thought he would hear. However, several seconds later he could make out a conversation. It was Deborah. But there was another voice too. It made sense to assume it was Shelby, since she has just spoken to him. But then again, time felt strange here; it was hard to keep track of it. If Shelby *had* spoken to him, that could have been hours or days ago. He waited to hear the voice again. Finally, the person spoke. It wasn't Shelby; it was a male voice—one too old to be his son.

"We're not where we'd like to be with this," the male voice said. Then it registered to Charles: this must be the voice of a doctor. "There was a lot of trauma to the head. He's just not responding like we would expect for someone in active recovery."

"What does that mean?" Deborah asked. Charles could tell by her voice that she was fighting hard to keep her composure and to sound like she was holding it together.

"It means we've got one more option to try," the doctor said. Charles tried to hear what the doctor was explaining, but suddenly his voice became muffled. After several seconds, though, the doctor's voice became clear enough to understand again. "It doesn't work all of the time, but we do have some success with it in patients who are in the same condition your husband is in."

"You don't sound very confident," Deborah said despairingly.

"I don't want to give you a false sense of hope, Mrs. Grey, I want to be realistic about this."

"But we should try this, right? If it were your spouse, what would you do?"

"I would try this, but I'd be realistic about it. I understand Mr. Grey is a pastor. My brother-in-law's a pastor too. I consider myself to be a person of faith. When I do this, I'm doing it with the understanding that this could really help. But ultimately, the outcome is determined on how hard your husband fights and the good Lord's healing touch."

"I understand. Let's do it then. Thank you, Doctor, for all you're doing. It means a lot."

"You're welcome. I wish I had better news. I'm sorry. I'll have to go downstairs and get all of the forms together, and someone will come up here in a bit and walk you through all of the details. We should be able to get this underway in the next few hours."

For a moment, Charles could hear mumbling again. The voices got harder to understand, and then silence filled the line, except for the noise of the machine and the occasional beep. Charles assumed that the doctor had left the room and he was alone with Deborah. He couldn't imagine how she was feeling right now. He wanted to hold her hand, to hug her, to comfort her in some way.

"God, let her know I'm here," Charles prayed. "Show her I'm not suffering."

Charles squeezed the receiver tightly and prayed again, asking God to comfort his wife and spare his life. After a moment he heard her again. "You just squeezed my hand! I knew you were still there. I love you so much, baby. Please hang in there. Please fight. There are so many people praying for you right now. Don't give up."

Then the line went back to the noise of the machine, but Charles thanked God for answering his prayer, at least part of it. While he didn't know how to fight harder, he would do his best to honor God with the next two guests who were to meet with him. Not feeling like going back to sleep, Charles got dressed in the clothes Ethel had washed and returned to him. Then he headed out of the room to whatever Bayou Refuge had in store for him.

CHAPTER 16

Charles could feel the mist of the fog settling on him. It was damp and cool, refreshing even. The sun cut through enough for him to see a familiar light on in the welcome center. He figured maybe Davy was there. He looked forward to catching up with his friend and telling him about his encounter with Tristan, as well as Ethel's struggle, the prior evening. Perhaps Davy might have some insight into what was going on with Ethel. Plus, he was sure Davy would want to hear about Tristan placing his faith in Jesus.

He walked into the welcome center and saw Davy wearing a red polo and khakis seated on one of the chairs with his legs propped up on a small ottoman. The worn fabric looked like something that came from the '80s, but it matched the style of the welcome center and the camp in general. Davy was, as expected, eating a biscuit with Ethel's blackberry jam, and a cup of coffee in a blue mug was set on a small table next to the chair.

"Good to see you, Charles," Davy said with a big smile. "Did you have a good evening?"

"It was interesting," Charles replied, then pointed to the biscuit and coffee. "Is there any more where that came from?"

Davy pointed to table that had a small plate of biscuits, homemade jam, a few coffee mugs, and a coffee pot with cream and sugar set next to it. "Help yourself. Plenty of it."

Charles grabbed a biscuit, put some jam on it, poured a mug of coffee, and then sat down in a chair across from Davy. He took a couple of bites of the biscuit, and it was perfection. As good as it was yesterday, the flavors somehow not only were exactly what he'd want them to be but it somehow made him think of all the conversations he had over the years while sitting with a cup of coffee and a biscuit. It caused him to get lost in the moment. He forced himself to set it down on the small table next to his chair and share about his conversation with Tristan. Davy listened intently as Charles retold how Tristan simply appeared in the café. Then he detailed his casual demeanor, how he had been hurt by his father and the church he grew up in, as well as his time in New Orleans. Finally, Charles shared how ultimately Tristan let go of his anger and hurt and gave his life to Christ.

"Then what happened?"

"He just disappeared!" Charles said. "Strangest thing ever! I looked all over the place and tried to catch a glimpse of him outside, but there wasn't a trace of him. Do you think he died?"

"Could have. If that's the case, at least he was ready," Davy said. "You ready for the next two guests?"

"Yeah, I think so," Charles responded. Then his mind turned back to his dream and the conversation he had heard his wife having with the doctor. He debated whether he should share this with Davy, but after struggling with it for a moment, he gave into the temptation. "I think I overheard a conversation that my wife was having with the doctor. It didn't sound good."

Davy made direct eye contact with Charles and gave him a soft, sympathetic smile in a way only a pastor could. He took his time gathering his thoughts before he spoke. "Kind of feels like this whole place is the valley of the shadow of death, huh? The Good Shepherd walks with us through those places too. You've walked with a lot of people as they've neared death, and you've shared encouragement from God's Word with them and helped them to get ready. Charles, I don't know what's going to come of this, but you ought to get yourself ready for whatever may come."

"It's just the thought of leaving my family and my church behind. I don't feel like they're ready," Charles replied. "This whole thing is so confusing and hard. I have these moments where I'm ready to let go and surrender to whatever God is going to do. But then I have other moments where the control freak inside of me wants to find something . . . *anything* that I can do to get out of this place and situation. I want to be ready for this. I want to be okay with whatever comes. I want to think that my family will be okay, but this is testing me in a way I've never been tested."

"None of us are ever one hundred percent ready for the loss of a loved one. But you were okay when you lost your dad. God took care of you, Charles. He put other people in your life to fill that role. Can you trust Him to do the same for your family and your church?"

"How are you so calm about this?" Charles asked frustratedly.

Davy leaned forward in his chair and smiled at Charles. "Charles, Jesus saved me I was in such a low, dark place. I had seen some things overseas during my service that jaded me. I honestly think if God hadn't saved me, I would have drunk myself to death and probably ruined the lives of my family. When I gave my life to Christ, I felt like I had seen the worst that this life had to offer. So I decided that if God would keep me from going back to what I was, I'd walk with Him no matter what. There are moments in life that have made me feel some of that old anger. Even here I've gotten frustrated! But God has kept me from going back to my old ways. One of the things that has helped me over the years when I've been in uncertain, chaotic seasons is asking God to help me trust in Him in every season—the one I'm in and the one to come. So I've been asking God to get me ready for this and to help me trust Him in every phase of life, including this one. When you feel yourself despairing, ask God to help you. Let the Holy Spirit work in your heart. Thank Him for all the joys you've had along the way, and consider how beautiful things will be in that sweet by and by. Whatever this is, it's just a season. It'll pass. There's something even more beautiful coming."

Charles took a sip of coffee and pondered Davy's words. Then he asked God to help him begin to accept whatever God had in store for him. To help him surrender the future of his family and church to his heavenly Father's divine hands.

The two sat drinking coffee and finishing their biscuits, both silently conversing with the Lord in their hearts. Charles for himself and Davy for Charles. Even though neither said anything, both were grateful for the other's presence. Finally, Charles broke the silence. "Hey Davy, something strange happened last night with Ethel. It was like she got weak all of a sudden. I thought she might pass out. Have you ever seen her do that before?"

"Hmm," Davy replied thoughtfully, scratching his chin.

"What could it mean? Do you have any idea?"

"Well," Davy began, then paused. "It could mean that her time here is drawing to an end."

Charles got up to fix himself another cup of coffee. He slowly poured it into the mug as he thought about what Davy had just said. He turned to ask another question but was surprised to see that Davy was no longer in his chair. Then he heard someone coming through the door. Charles expected to see Davy; instead, he saw a woman who appeared to be in her late thirties with short brown hair dressed in stylish blue jeans, a red blouse, and a white cardigan that hung down several inches past her waist. Silver earrings dangled from her ears, and a necklace with a silver locket hung from her neck. She had a brown overnight bag hanging from her shoulder and was looking at her cell phone, which sat in a dainty sunflower case. She appeared visibly shook. Charles assumed it was from the lack of a cell signal.

"Am I in the right place?" she asked, giving Charles a quick glance before looking back down at her phone.

CHAPTER 17

The immediate switch from Davy to this woman startled Charles, and it took himself a minute to gather his bearings. He had gone from the shock of Davy disappearing to the sudden arrival of what he could only assume to be was the next guest. He'd had no opportunity to prepare. In his mind, he was hoping to engage in conversation with her either over lunch or supper in the café, not in the welcome center. He walked over to greet her properly and wanted to call her by name. Did Davy say her name? Charles couldn't remember. Connor always gave him a hard time about remembering names. As a pastor, he talked to a lot of people. Some of them he saw every week and knew quite well; others he only saw on occasion and struggled to remember their names. Connor could tell by his face when he had forgotten a name and would make sure later that he let his father know that he was getting old.

"Come on! It's up there somewhere, old man." He could hear his son saying.

He smiled at the woman and began to think frantically. Charles thought he remembered that it started with a *C* or a *K*. Was it Carla? No. Carly? That didn't seem right either. Kim didn't feel right, but it seemed closer. Then it rushed into his mind.

"Would you be Kayla?" he asked warmly.

"The one and only," she replied with a sweet smile.

"That's great! I'm Charles. It's nice to meet you. Feel free to set your bag down and sit if you'd like."

"Sure," Kayla responded as she set her bag down on the ground and took a seat on the couch that Davy had been seated on a few minutes ago. "Nice eighties vibe going on here. I like the retro feel. Looks like a church camp my friends dragged me to one time when I was a kid."

"Would you like a cup of coffee? There's also some biscuits," Charles offered as he motioned to the refreshments.

"I'll take some coffee, but I'll pass on the biscuits. And Stevia and a little cream if you have it."

Charles walked over to the coffee pot, poured some coffee in an old Bayou Refuge coffee mug, and then poured in some cream as well. "I don't have sugar substitute, just sugar. Is that okay?"

"No, I'll pass. I'm on a program, so I can't do sugar. I'll just take cream." Kayla tapped on her cell phone with frustration. "I just upgraded this thing, and it's not working right. How far is the nearest Target? Wait, that's a stupid question. Sorry, how far is the nearest Dollar General? I'll need to grab some Stevia and a few other things."

Charles hesitated, not sure of what to say. "Oh, it's down a little ways. But until that fog lifts, no one's going anywhere."

"I'm not scared of a little fog. My car has all the bells and whistles. It'll keep me safe on the road," Kayla responded. "What is up with the signal here? This is crazy. Can you give me the Wi-Fi password?"

Charles handed her the cup of coffee and sat down in a chair across from her. I'm sorry, but we're just getting everything back up and running here. There's no Wi-Fi at the moment." Charles thought for a minute about how to break away her attention from her defunct phone and move toward more important topics. "Do you have any children?"

"Three kids: Joshua, Kevin, and Eva. My husband graciously volunteered to cover for me so that I could come to this getaway that my doctor is saying I have to take. But he has no clue how to get all of the kids where they need to be. Joshua has band practice and soccer after school, but in between those he's got to bring Kevin to violin practice and Eva to her dance practice. Then he needs to help Joshua finish his science project. Kevin has a math test he needs help preparing for tonight, and Eva is supposed to bring cupcakes to class tomorrow. He said he will bake her cupcakes and for me not to worry about it. But let me tell you how my husband bakes. He will run to Walmart and get two boxes of premade cupcakes, and then the other moms are going to give me a hard time about it the next time we're together. I can hear Lila now, *That stuff has too many chemicals! You know you shouldn't let your kids eat that stuff.*"

Charles put his head down and tried to hide a smile because on more than one occasion, his definition of bringing a dessert had consisted of grabbing a store-bought pie or cake. His mind raced to get a handle on the situation. Most of his encounters with people on Seekers Weekends at Bayou Refuge over the years consisted of people who seemed to have a desire to think more about spiritual matters. They came here *seeking*. While Tristan may not have come to Bayou Refuge as a typical seeker, he was aware that he was close to death and was open to having a spiritual conversation. Kayla was different. Charles prayed in his heart that God would open a door for discussion because he wasn't even sure if this woman was aware that she was dying. At least, that was the only reason he could think of her being here. If all of this was even real. Kalya seemed to finally get aggravated and put her phone away in the bag. She looked at it with a hint of sadness, like she had lost a friend.

"I'm sorry," Kayla said, looking back at him. "I'm afraid I'm not very good without my phone. I like to shop, text, read, and check emails or social media. I feel useless when I can't do anything. I guess maybe being out of signal for a little while can't be a bad thing. I'll check on the crew when I sneak out to the Dollar General later."

Not feeling like it was the right time to correct her, Charles simply gave her a smile and a nod.

"Coffee's good," Kayla said as she looked into her mug. "I usually can't do very much without some sweetener in it, but this blend must have some sweetness roasted into it or something. Tastes like it came from that little French coffee shop in Baton Rouge."

"You said you had been to a church camp before. Was it somewhere that reminded you of this place?" Charles said, hoping to steer the conversation to a spiritual discussion.

"I have! One somewhere around Eunice maybe," Kayla replied. "I honestly don't remember much about it. I think a friend invited me, and my mom and dad were all too eager to get rid of me for a week."

"Did you go to church any growing up?" Charles asked.

"No, never as a family unless someone died or was getting married, or if there was some sort of big event going on where my parents could drop me off for a while and not have to worry about me. They were always very . . . into themselves. It's not like they were mean parents or anything. They just always had stuff going on. I was the only child and always felt like I was trying to stay out of the way." After a few seconds she cleared her throat as if to hold back a tear. "I am so sorry. This is not who I am. I do not open up to strangers about my life. Please forgive me. Is there like some sort of schedule for the next . . . Hmm, how long is this *thing* going to go?"

Something was happening. Charles could see it in Kayla's face. She was starting to have some of the same moments of confusion that Charles had had over the last couple of days. He remembered how overwhelming the whole experience had been and wanted to show her the same kindness Davy had shown him.

"Are you okay?" Charles asked in a calm way in an attempt to give her some freedom to think out loud or ask for clarification if she needed any.

"I'm sorry, but I'm not feeling like myself. I'm having trouble keeping some things straight in my mind. I remember waking up this morning. I was getting ready to go to work when I nodded off. I never do that, but I've been having some . . ." She paused for a few seconds as if trying not to say the wrong thing or reveal too much information. "I've been having some stress issues. They've been watching my heart recently. It's a condition I've had since childhood. Trust me, it's a long, boring story. I remembered my husband telling me that he was making me get away, that I never stop. In fact, last night we fought about it. He told me this morning he was going to set up a get-away for me. Then I got the call from the doctor saying a retreat was set up here and I had been scheduled. This just feels rushed and doesn't make a lot of sense," Kayla said, confused by her own words. Then she put her head down and rubbed her forehead. "I'm really tired. Would it be possible to go and lay down in my room for a little while?"

"Sure, let me grab your bag." Charles reached down, grabbed her brown bag, and helped her up. As the two began to head out the door, Charles noticed that Claude and Ethel were standing there.

"Hello, dear," Ethel said. "So glad you've arrived."

"Let us take the bag on over and get her situated," Claude said, taking the bag. "Go back and have another cup of coffee. Ethel will have lunch set up when the two of you are ready."

Kayla gave Charles a polite nod and walked off with the elderly couple.

As they stepped off into the distance, he overheard Kayla say, "You know, you look so much like my grandmother. You could have been her sister."

CHAPTER 18

Charles fixed himself another cup of coffee, realizing that this was his third cup. He was about to fuss at himself for drinking too much, but then he realized it probably didn't matter how much of it he drank in this place. In fact, he couldn't remember even going to the bathroom since he'd been here. He tried not to think about that too much though. He walked over to a large window with a good view to the bayou and enjoyed a moment of prayer while he admired the scenery. It was still the same as it had been since he came here. A heavy fog allowed him to only see a little ways out, almost like it surrounded the camp, but wasn't too thick in the actual camp. Like it was isolating this place. He let his mind wonder what would happen if he up and walked through the fog and left Bayou Refuge. Where would he go? Would he just wind up right back here regardless of where he went? Or what if by leaving he could force himself to wake up?

His mind didn't stay in this direction of thought very long because something caught his eye: the rapid movement of a small creature on the edge of the bayou next to a pair of old wooden rocking chairs set out there for reflecting and for the occasional fisherman.

"What in the world?" Charles said, wondering what this next surprise would bring.

He hadn't seen a bird or an animal since he'd come here. He couldn't figure out what it was. Maybe a small deer or a dog based on its size. He looked around again but for the life of him couldn't see it. His eyes scanned every tree and bush, but nothing. Charles was just about to give up looking, thinking that maybe his eyes were playing tricks on him, when he saw it again. But this time it wasn't running; it was walking slowly on two legs. He squinted his eyes and could tell it was a person, but oddly enough it wasn't Claude, Ethel, Davy, or Kayla. It was a small boy in an old pair of denim overalls. Based on the child's height, he couldn't be more than six or seven years old.

Was this the third person Charles was supposed to talk to? Did they happen to show up at the same time. Then the thought hit him. If there was a child here, and this place was real, it meant that there was a child back in the real world who wasn't doing well. The thought took Charles's breath away. It wasn't that he didn't know that children suffered and died all of the time; it just wasn't an easy thought to process. He figured he was supposed to talk with the child, so he said a quick prayer and prepared himself to try and encourage this little one.

Charles made his way out of the welcome center cabin and slowly walked to where the rocking chairs were. However, when he made the corner, the child had vanished yet again. There was no little boy in denim overalls standing by the rockers—just empty chairs. One of them rocked back and forth in a steady fashion as if to indicate that it had been occupied only a moment earlier. Charles looked all around him and even walked completely around the cabin but saw no trace of the child. When he circled the front, he could see Claude and Ethel making their way back to their house. Without even thinking about it, he yelled out, "Hey, guys! Have y'all seen a child walking around?"

The couple stopped walking and turned to around to face Charles. Claude looked at Ethel with a slight smile, and she returned a smile to him, as if the older couple was in on some sort of joke that Charles had never heard. "Well, Charles, all sorts of folks come and go around here. Usually not very many come at once, but we see all sorts of folks," Claude said.

The comment perplexed Charles because it felt like they knew who he was talking about, based on their smiles, but they didn't want to tell him. Not in a menacing way, but like they didn't want to spoil anything. He wasn't sure what to think about that. "Well, did you see a child today?"

"No, I don't think we have, dear," Ethel replied. "However, if he's here you'll see him when he's ready. I wouldn't worry about it. Might be worth getting a little rest before lunch. I'm sure you've got an interesting conversation in front of you."

"Yes, ma'am," Charles replied. "Thank you."

Charles then turned and walked toward the cabin and figured that, like everything else here so far, it would all make sense when it was supposed to.

CHAPTER 19

He fell into a dream-filled sleep. He was seated on an old carpeted floor and saw Deborah, but she looked younger. Her dark-brown hair looked fuller, and there was a certain youthfulness to her when she smiled that he hadn't seen in a long time. Not that he didn't absolutely adore the woman she had become, but he hadn't seen her quite like this in years. She was wearing a black top that looked in fashion years ago. Thinking about how good she looked in it put a smile on his face. Upon a closer look, he could tell that she was a bit larger in the midsection. His mind turned to when they had been here at Bayou Refuge when she was pregnant with Shelby some fourteen years ago. He looked around the room and noticed a board game spread out in front of them. He recognized it as an old trivia game they used to play. Deborah was never any good at it but loved playing it, so he used to guess incorrectly on purpose just to drag out the game a bit more to make her feel better. Next to the board was a box of chocolate chip cookies, a bag of potato chips, and a couple of cans of orange soda.

This felt identical to that night. If you made him put together a top-ten list of favorite dates, this would have been one of them. They had just gone through a challenging season of ministry and life. For a while, it had felt like everything around them that could go wrong went wrong. Money was tight, her mom was battling cancer, and Charles had been hurt by a dear friend at church who was upset with him and had spread some rumors about him. However, Deborah made them get away. They didn't have much, but she was adamant that before the baby came, the two of them were going to have one more special weekend. Deborah had dropped off Connor at her sister's house and was ready to head out as soon as Charles got in from the office that day. As much as he wasn't looking forward to the get-away, he ended up loving it. He enjoyed watching his wife laugh and have a good time. She made his whole world seem brighter. It seemed that no matter what he faced, if she was there with him, he was able to face it. Being with her like this was a gift from God. It strengthened and encouraged him in a special way. Charles knew it was just a dream, but it felt so real. There was something special about being back in this moment with her that touched his heart. He watched her laugh and cut up as she tried to answer some question about hedgehogs, then her laughter turned to surprise. He knew what was coming. She grabbed his hand and put it on her belly. He smiled as he felt his daughter kick.

"Are you ready for your little girl?" Deborah asked, then leaned over and kissed his cheek. Charles basked in that moment, never wanting it to end.

"Can we stay here in this moment forever?" Charles asked. He was certain he hadn't asked it that night so many years ago, but he was asking now. The desire for control and to get a handle on this situation was overwhelming him. Here, this place, in this moment, it was all he wanted.

Deborah looked at him in the way that only a wife who was trying to respond encouragingly to her husband can. She hesitated for a moment, gathering her thoughts. Charles could imagine that in her desire to keep him close—even if this was all in his imagination—Deborah would want nothing more than to be here with him now, reliving this scene. However, she tilted her head a bit and grabbed his hand, then interlocked her fingers with his and squeezed them tight, speaking as if she was going to say something she didn't want to.

"Charles, if we stay in this moment, as good as it is, never leaving it, then think about all the great things God has for us that we will have to miss."

"I don't want to leave you. I'm scared to. I know I tell people to be courageous and trust in God, but I don't want to right now. I just want you, this," Charles said, surprised by the desperation in his own voice.

"This moment right here? It's forever ours, locked into the mind of God for all eternity. Nothing can undo it. We don't know what comes next in all of this. But I know it's okay if you have to go because in light of eternity, it won't be long until we're back together forever again," Deborah said slowly but confidently. "I'll be okay, and the kids will be okay. Don't you worry about us.

You've set us up well to be ready in our hearts for whatever life brings."

Then it was over. Charles was alone, back in the room again by himself. Tears rolled down his cheeks, and he didn't even make an attempt to stop them. He knew it was just a dream, but it felt like she had been there. It was sweet and tragic at the same time. He sat up in bed, said a prayer, and tried to clear his mind. He felt a growling in his stomach, like he was hungry. He figured that now would be as good time as any to make his way over to the café and see if Kayla had shown up for lunch yet.

CHAPTER 20

Charles arrived at the café just in time to find Ethel setting up the last of the meal. A large pot of gumbo had been placed on the serving table, and next to it a large bowl of rice, along with potato salad and French bread. At the end of the table was a large pitcher of sweet tea and a bowl of banana pudding. Charles noticed a small dining table for Kayla and him to sit. Ethel was moving and adjusting the layout of everything on the table to make sure it was just to her liking. There was something encouraging in the way that Ethel took serving food as serious as Charles took the conversations he was having with people as a minister both here and back home. Perhaps Ethel and Claude believed that if they could put someone at ease and make them more open to a conversation about Christ, then all of the effort was worthwhile. Certainly in Charles's mind it was. Plus, the smell of fresh gumbo filling the room made Charles feel much more at ease.

"Looks great," Charles said. "And it smells great too."

"I talked to Kayla a few minutes ago. She said she was feeling better and would be making her way here shortly. It's hard getting here, you know. It takes us all a little time to relax. I think she is still very confused, but she's at ease now and hopefully ready to talk," Ethel said.

"I hope so too," Charles said. Based on what Ethel was saying, it implied that she understood, in some way, what this place was. "Are you feeling better today?"

"Oh, sure. I'll be fine. It's just one of those things," Ethel said. "Don't you worry about this old gal. Good Lord's going to take care of me. I'm moving a little slower today, but I'm sure I'll be fine."

"I appreciate all of your work here, Ethel. It means a lot to me, and I'm sure it does to others."

She looked at him with a soft smile, revealing a bit of sadness. Then she looked down at the blue dress she was wearing and at the white walking shoes on her feet as if to gather her thoughts, then she looked back at Charles. "We all just do the best we can until our very last breath. And we do it all for the Lord. But I do appreciate the encouragement. It is good to see you again."

"Anything that I can help with?" Charles asked, certain that there wouldn't be.

"Not a thing! I think I've gotten it all taken care of. Now I just need to get back to the house and make sure Claude stops and eats lunch."

She made her final adjustments and then nodded at Charles and headed out of the room. Charles got up to fix himself a glass of tea and had just sat down at the table when Kayla entered the café. She looked a bit more relaxed and a little less flustered than when they had met at the welcome center earlier. The white sweater and red blouse looked slightly wrinkled, as if she had slept in her clothes.

"Good to see you again," Charles said. "Did you get a little rest?"

"I did. This smells wonderful. I feel like I'm back at my grandma's house. She used to make the best gumbo. You know, my husband and I have traveled all over, and I've eaten food from so many different places, but it's funny that some of the food I crave the most is hers. I never thought to learn to cook it when she was alive. Life's funny like that."

"I've never eaten anything from Ethel that wasn't great. Fix yourself a bowl," Charles said, motioning to the food. She made her way over to the pot and stopped to take in the smell of it when she opened the lid.

"Oh, this is gonna be great," she said as she fixed herself a bowl. "I never do rice, but I think I might today. And this potato salad looks awesome." She set down her bowl of gumbo and plate of potato salad at the table and then went to get some tea.

"Is this sweet tea? I'm really trying to get in shape for . . ." She trailed off and paused a moment. "You know what? It doesn't matter today." She poured herself a glass of sweet tea and took her seat at the table. Charles followed suit, fixing himself a bowl, along with potato salad, French bread, and a glass of tea and then asked if he could bless the food. The request caught Kayla off guard.

With a mouth full of potato salad, she nodded her head yes. They both bowed their heads and closed their eyes.

"God, we thank you for this food and for the opportunity to eat and fellowship together. Would you bless this food, bless Mrs. Ethel for fixing it, and bless this time together? In Jesus' name we pray, amen."

"I'm sorry," Kayla said. "I didn't know we were doing that here. I hope I didn't offend you."

"Not at all. You said your grandmother was a good cook. Did you get to spend a lot of time with her growing up?"

Kayla took a sip of tea to wash down her food, then cleared her throat. "Yeah, some. The only grandmother I knew was on my mom's side, and she and my dad didn't get along. Dad didn't care to have much to do with her, so we didn't see her often. But she'd call and pester them enough that during the summer and on the holidays I'd go over there some. She'd cook for me, and we'd play card games and dominos. Grandpa was a farmer, so he'd always want me to ride with him on the tractor and look at his fields. Those were definitely good times."

"Sounds like it," Charles replied. The two ate in silence for a moment. Charles prayed in his heart for some guidance to turn the conversation to spiritual matters, not knowing if this might be the last chance this woman had to get things right with God.

"Tell me about yourself," Kayla said.

"Well, I'm a Louisiana native. I have a wonderful wife named Deborah, two great kids, a seventh grader named Shelby, and a sophomore in high school named Connor. I pastor a small church about an hour and a half down the road from here, and I enjoy retreats like these where I get to talk with people about spiritual things," Charles said, realizing that the last part had been blurted out in the least smooth way possible.

"Spiritual things?" Kayla said with a nervous laugh. "Why would my husband and doctor sign me up for a spiritual retreat?"

"I don't know. Of course, we don't have to talk about it if you don't want to, but sometimes when we're looking at stress and physical health issues, there can be a lot of value in stopping to think about spiritual things."

Kayla pushed her plate away and gave Charles a bit of a mischievous look. He had no idea what she was thinking. After a few seconds she finally spoke. "You're a preacher, so what happens here has to stay in confidence, right?"

"Yeah," Charles said, not sure where the conversation was headed. "That's normally how this works."

"I'll make a deal with you. I'm going to get a big bowl of that banana pudding and another glass of this sweet tea. You won't tell a soul I ate dessert, and I'll listen to your thoughts on spiritual things," Kayla said with a playful smile.

"I think I can do that." Charles appreciated her openness to the conversation and the bit of fun she seemed to be having with him.

"Want a bowl?" she asked as she got up and headed over to the dessert.

"Sure, it would hit the spot after this gumbo."

A moment later Kayla returned, carefully carrying a bowl for each of them as well as another glass of sweet tea. She sat down and began to eat her dessert. Charles took a bite of his and although it tasted phenomenal, his mind was on how to segue the conversation. After a few seconds, he figured he'd just ask a question and see where she was spiritually.

"Kayla, what do you think about God?"

"Direct, are we?" Kayla replied as she took another bite of pudding. "I don't know, Charles. I won't claim to have it all figured out. I guess, spiritually speaking, I'm just not very focused on God or anything like that now. I had a crappy childhood. So my mind and my focus is on giving my kids what I couldn't have and enjoying a bit of life myself. With three kids and a husband who keeps me busy enough, when I'm not rushing them from practice to practice, shopping, cooking dinner, or doing something for my husband, I'm either decompressing on social media or with whatever television series me and my husband like at the moment. We don't really do the church thing. I've got nothing against it, just different things for different people. I figure if I'm doing my thing and I'm not hurting anyone, God's not gonna be too worried about me."

"I appreciate the honesty," Charles said.

"I don't mean to belittle you or what you do. I just don't really want this spiritual stuff right now. If I had known that's what this thing was, I would have stayed home."

"You don't ever think about there being more than this life?"

"Honestly, I try not to. I'm sure when the kids are grown that's a rabbit hole I might spend some time exploring."

"What if you wait until it's too late?"

"How mean would that be of God to take me out before I had a chance to get right with Him?" Kayla asked haughtily. "Besides, I always figured that if He really wanted something to do with me, He would have let me know by now. He's so out there and distant. If it mattered He'd say it to me in a way that would get me to listen."

"Well, what if He is trying to get your attention right now? Maybe that's why He has you here."

Kayla pushed her bowl away and leaned back in her chair, looking more intensely at Charles, indicating that she really was trying to engage in this conversation. "No, this is a error on my husband's part. I shouldn't even be here. This is not who I am. I can find my solace in a glass of wine after a nice meal, or shopping online for an outfit. I don't need there to be a God. And if there is one, I really don't need Him to care about me. Sure, I'm not perfect. I've got a couple of maxed out credit cards my husband doesn't know about, and I'm not always fully transparent about staying on top of my heart exams. But come on! There's no despair or emptiness here."

"Kayla, do you believe the Bible?" Charles asked, trying to switch up the conversation a bit.

"I guess, to some degree," she said, a bit relieved to talk about the philosophy of the Bible and not her need for God. "I took a religions course in college, and Christianity definitely makes more sense to me than other religions. Multiple authors, inspired by God over thousands of years in agreement with each other and all that."

"I'm impressed," Charles said. "So you've read it?"

Kayla smiled and laughed a little. "A little here and there. I guess you'd think I would have read more after saying something like that."

"If you believe it's inspired by God, then why haven't you read it all?" Charles asked.

Kayla rubbed the table with her hands for a few seconds. Then she pushed her chair back and crossed her legs. "I guess because I don't really want to."

"The truth about eternal life, the truth about God's love for you and how to receive it is right there. Is that worth receiving?" Charles asked.

"Charles, no offense to you or to God, or to whoever else, but I want to live my life on my own terms. I want to give my kids the world that I never got. I want to travel with my husband and experience all sorts of things that this world has to offer. At some point I'm probably going to "find" God. But it'll be on my time," Kayla said with a firm tone. "I appreciate what you're doing here but—"

"Kayla, think about how you got here," Charles interrupted in a calm but direct way, hating to take the conversation here but not knowing what else to do. "Think about all of the details of this place. You said earlier today there were some things that were confusing."

"What are you saying?"

"You said you were having health problems. You said you fell asleep this morning, and when you woke up you vaguely remember coming here, correct?"

"Yeah, I guess that's right."

"You wondered why there were no other people here. You even said a few minutes ago that you thought that it was strange that your husband sent you to a religious retreat," Charles added, almost spelling it out for her.

"I don't understand."

Charles didn't respond to her comment. He simply prayed in his heart that God would help her piece some things together. He knew that if he came out and said the words directly, it might be too much for her to accept. However, if she said them herself, she might believe them. He remembered how he had felt when he began to put the pieces of his puzzle together. After several seconds he could hear Kayla talking quietly to herself. She grabbed her cup and walked over to the table with the pitcher of tea and refilled her glass.

"The tea, the gumbo, the potato salad," Kayla said quietly. "It tastes so much like my grandmother's cooking that it's unreal."

"Everything I've had here has been wonderful too," Charles said, choosing his words carefully. "Perfect."

"It's all too perfect!" Kayla added. "It feels like a weird dream. The fog shows no signs of lifting. I have no cell signal. I saw no people on the way out here, just somehow rode through the fog and got here. I barely remember it. Then I slept, in the middle of the day, passed out for hours. I've never done that before. I dreamed I was there with my kids and husband, vacationing on the beach like we did a few years back. It was so real. You ever had a dream like that?"

"I have. In fact, I had one earlier this morning," Charles said, trying not to think about it too much, afraid it would bring the tears back to his eyes.

"I'm going to ask a weird question," Kayla said. "Just humor me."

"Okay," Charles replied, curious to see where she was taking the conversation. "I can do that."

"Is this place real?" She walked over to the table and sat back down.

"I honestly am not sure. I think it is, just not *real* like how we normally think of it."

"What do you mean?"

"Kayla, yesterday morning I left my house and went to a meeting. Then something *happened* while I was on the road. I am becoming convinced that I was in a car accident on the way here and that's why I'm at Bayou Refuge," Charles explained. He watched her trying to put the pieces together in her head.

"Are you saying we're dead?" she asked matter-of-factly.

"I don't think so. But I do think this is some sort of place we go to when our bodies are dying but our brains haven't shut down yet. I think God brought you here for a reason."

"So I'm not dead?" Kayla asked.

"No, I don't think so," Charles replied reassuringly. "I've had moments where it feels like I'm hearing my family members talking about me or to me, and I think I've heard them having conversations with doctors. So it feels like my brain is still absorbing some of that information. But I'm not fully there; part of me is here. I know, it sounds weird to say it."

"I can't believe it! I'm supposed to go every six months and get a couple of heart tests. But the hospital is out of town and a hassle to go to. And since I'd never had any heart issues as an adult, I started using my 'good health' as an excuse to go on a little get-away for the day. Sometimes I'd even spend the night and convince my husband that the tests were so early in the morning it made more sense to stay overnight. I'd have some 'me time.' You know, with all the kids' programs and his work schedule, it was a little time for me to unwind. My general practitioner was worried about these spells I was having, but I wasn't I had anxiety issues in high school and these felt just like that. Honestly, I just thought it was that and all I needed to do was relax, nothing some shopping therapy couldn't handle.. I lied and told him all the heart tests were fine. That I just needed to find some time to unwind and I'd be better. I'm such an idiot. I can't believe this is happening!" Kayla said angrily.

Charles was grateful Kayla was beginning to understand what might be happening. He waited in silence to see if she'd calm down.

"Well, if we're still alive and conscious, there has to be a way back," Kayla said with a bit of excitement in her voice. "Maybe if we go through the fog, we can leave this place. I don't want to stay here. No offense, but I want to get back to my family. There's got to be some way to fight this."

"I don't think this is that kind of situation. There's nothing to fight. We have no control over what's happening out there. But we can make sure that our hearts are right with the Lord in case we don't get to go back, in case we leave here and go into eternity," Charles said firmly, hoping she would consider the importance of what he was saying.

Kayla got up, clearly becoming panicked, pulled on her sweater, and began to pace. She looked as if she was trying to figure out some puzzle. Charles stayed silent for a moment, trusting she would choose wisely. Kayla continued to pace, stopping a time or two, then going right back to it. "Kayla why don't you sit back down and think about something. God loves you and is giving you this chance, one that a lot of people probably don't have. He's giving you a chance to consider what Christ did for you on the cross. You can receive that love. You can give your life to Him and make your heart right with God and know that whatever happens, you're going to be okay."

She remained silent, but she stopped pacing and looked intently at Charles. He continued sharing his heart with her. "The

Bible tells us that once sin entered the world, all of creation was messed up and broken. That includes us. People are broken. We have broken families. We see the impact of brokenness all around us. We try to fix that brokenness on our own but we can't. Our attempts don't work. Often, they just mess us up more. But the good news is that God sent His Son, Jesus, to come and live a perfect life and die on the cross for our sins. We've got to turn from our sins and believe that Jesus died on the cross for us and rose from the grave. Does this make sense, Kayla?" Charles had shared the gospel many times in his life, but he had never shared it with this much intensity. He knew in his mind that this was Kayla's last chance. For another moment she didn't break her gaze, then she turned and shook her head.

"I told you, Charles, that I would deal with this spiritual stuff when I'm old and gray, not while my kids are still in the house, not while I've got so many other things to focus on. You can sit here and let yourself die, but I'm fighting this. I'm going back," Kayla said in a loud, angry voice. She turned and headed to the door of the café.

Charles rose to his feet and made his way to the door. He had to stop her. He had to get her to reconsider. She needed to listen. "Kayla, don't do this! I know this is hard, but don't walk away. Please give this more thought!"

She stopped at the white door, her hand resting on the handle, and looked Charles in the eyes. "This stuff is not for me. Leave me alone!" Then she turned and walked out of the door, making a point to slam it behind her.

CHAPTER 21

Charles rushed to the door and opened it to see that night had fallen even though it didn't feel like they had been in the café that long. He looked around frantically to see which direction Kayla had gone, but he couldn't see her anywhere. His stomach dropped, or at least that's what it felt like. She was gone. He walked around the building and yelled her name. He looked for her like he had never looked for anything in his life before because he didn't want to think about her being separated from God. In his desperation he walked through the library, the welcome center and knocked on every door of the cabin where she was staying. Charles wasn't ready to give up on their conversation.

"Kayla!" he yelled repeatedly.

He was convinced that if he wasn't in this place and back in his old life, that his voice would have been hoarse and his throat sore. After several minutes he began to feel himself weaken. In his heart he knew what had happened. Kayla had left, not only the café, but this existence. She must have died in the real world. Maybe she woke up, but in his heart he doubted that.

After walking the whole center he stood near the exterior of the café door and saw a familiar silhouette approach him and was unsure where it came from or how long it had been there. Charles felt angry. Angry at himself and angry at God for not giving this woman more of a chance. Still, a part of him was glad to see the old man. Davy approached him in the standard attire: red polo and khakis.

"Where is she, Davy?" Charles asked in desperation.

"She's gone, son. She made her choice," Davy said with sympathy in his voice for both Charles and for Kayla. "There's nothing else we can do."

Charles wanted to say a lot, but it was so jumbled together in his mind that he couldn't get his words out. So he just put his head down and tried to get his bearings. He wished the fog would consume him. In this moment, he had no desire to be here. He felt useless, and all he wanted was to go back home or to move on to glory, yet he could do neither. All he could do was stand here on this strange, foggy plane of existence, thinking about what went wrong. He felt a hand on his shoulder. Davy was wise enough to know when words wouldn't suffice. Charles thought of Job's friends. Even they were a comfort until they opened their mouths. It didn't seem like anyone could say anything in this moment that would make him feel better, but it was nice to know he wasn't alone.

The two men stood in silence for a while, then Charles began to walk. Davy walked next to him—not saying a word, just being a friendly presence. It made Charles think of the Lord's faithful presence even when we don't understand what He is doing. He's still close, walking with us through whatever situation we face. Just as Davy was with Charles, Charles also knew that God was with him. He knew God didn't care that he was mad at Him in this moment. God loved him anyway. There was something peaceful and reassuring in that.

They made their way to the edge of the bayou. Charles stared out across the water, past the cypress trees and into the fog, wanting to see that little island where the cross was, just like the picture in his room. Though all he could see was the trees, the water, and the fog. After what felt like hours but may have only been a few minutes, he began to feel very tired. So much so that he was struggling to keep his eyes open. He looked at Davy and said, "I think I need to go lie down. I'm feeling really tired."

Davy patted Charles on the back and smiled a little. "That's probably a good idea. Sometimes that's the most spiritual thing we can do, you know? Just close our eyes and let God be God. Let me walk you back to the cabin."

"Thank you," Charles replied. Even though it was only two words, Charles was attempting to express a deep level of gratitude for all Davy had done not only in this moment but over the years, and Davy was fully aware of his gratitude. The two men turned and headed through the darkness to the cabin.

CHAPTER 22

Charles didn't even remember lying down and going to sleep, but suddenly he awoke to the sound of a giggle. At first, he thought he was back home and was hearing his daughter laugh as she tried to mess with him first thing in the morning—something that she did from time to time. But then he remembered where he was, and his mind went from relaxed to frantic and confused. In one swift motion he threw the covers off, opened his eyes, and sat up. It only took him a moment to see the little boy he had seen outside by the rocking chairs. He was dressed in blue overalls with a white undershirt and held a red ball. The little boy could have been no older than six or seven with dirty-blond buzz-cut hair. The child smiled at him as if he had found a new friend.

Charles had to admit that he really didn't know how to respond. It was certainly strange to have the child in his room. Plus, the idea of a child in this place was a bit hard to wrap his mind around. What did it mean? However, after the events of the previous evening, Charles decided that he wasn't ready to think about this too much. Then the thought occurred to him: maybe this was the third person he was supposed to talk to about Jesus. He was a little young, but Charles had seen children at this age place their faith in Jesus. However, the thought of having his final conversation made him fearful for what would come after that. Would he wake up with his family or enter into eternity?

"Are you Mr. Charles?" the little boy asked as he tossed his small red ball up in the air and attempted to catch it. He missed, however, and the ball fell to the ground and rolled toward the door. When the little boy walked over to get it, Charles noticed the child's lack of shoes and it made him smile. All nervous thoughts disappeared from Charles' mind and he felt more relaxed than he had at any point during his stay at Bayou Refuge. The child's peace and happiness was somehow contagious.

"I am," Charles replied. "What's your name?"

"I'm Kendall," the little boy said. "But everyone calls me Kenny."

"Well, Kenny, it's nice to meet you. But what are you doing in my room? Am I supposed to talk to you?"

Kenny laughed as if he had just heard a joke. "No, silly. I'm supposed to talk to you. My buddy said I'm gonna hang out with you today."

"What do you mean?" Charles asked as he walked over to where his shoes were and put them on. He realized that he had never changed out of what he was wearing last night and didn't really see the need to right now. His mind was more set on understanding what Kenny's response.

"Let's see . . ." Kenny said with his finger raised up to his lips as if he was deep in thought. "It's like I have to play with you because you're sad. You're supposed to help other people, but now I'm gonna help you."

Had God really sent this child to put Charles at ease after the failed conversation he had had with Kayla? As angry as Charles had been with the Lord the night before, now he was struggling not to cry because God, in His love, sent someone to encourage him. As unfair as it had seemed to him last night that Kayla was whisked off to eternity, it seemed just as unfair now that God would show this kind of love to Charles.

"You excited?" Kenny said as he pointed to Charles like an MC seeking a reaction from the crowd.

"Sure, Kenny. What are we going to do?

"Let's go play," Kenny said. As quick as the words were out of his mouth, the little fellow ran out of the door. "Come on!"

Charles had to pick up his pace to keep up with Kenny, but he had to admit he liked the challenge of it. He followed the little boy down the cabin hallway, through the door, and out onto the grounds of Bayou Refuge. When Charles looked around, it felt like even though the fog was still there, the light was coming through it a little more. This felt like the brightest he had seen the camp since he had gotten there. However, he hardly had time to take it in because Kenny stopped and yelled, "Catch!" Then, at what felt like lightning speed, the red ball Kenny had been holding and tossing flew toward Charles. He raised his hand up as quick as he could and still almost missed it.

"Got quite the arm on you, huh?" Charles said with a big grin. This felt just like playing ball with his own son. It didn't make him feel sad but at ease, almost like he was home. He tossed the ball back at Kenny, maybe a bit faster than he should have, but Kenny had no problem catching it and laughed when he did. The two stood there and tossed the ball for what seemed to be twenty or thirty minutes. After a while Kenny decided to run past Charles when he caught it, like a football player trying to get past the defensive line. It seemed that Kenny had chosen a particular tree as an end zone. Sometimes Charles would let him run past him; other times Charles would playfully pick up the little fellow, run him back a few yards, then set him down. The game continued like that for a while.

The two of them were quite lost in play and didn't notice Claude and Ethel sitting there on their porch, watching the two run around with big smiles on their faces. Neither did they notice Davy standing by another tree doing the same. It wasn't until Kenny put the ball in his pocket and ran up to tap Charles and instigate a game of tag that Charles noticed the others. Charles chased Kenny toward Davy, who used his large build to stand in front of Kenny and allow Charles a chance to catch him. Kenny was laughing like a child on Christmas morning. Charles tapped the boy and ran behind a skinny tree and acted like he was hiding. Kenny thought it was the funniest thing in the world and wasted no time in going to tap Charles and then doing the same thing.

Tag turned into hide-and-seek, which turned into racing, which turned into skipping rocks. After they skipped rocks into the bayou for a while, Kenny looked over at Charles and Davy, who had walked over to try to show both the child and Charles the proper technique, and said, "I'm hungry I think I could eat."

"I think we can handle that. Don't you, Ethel?" Claude said. Claude and Ethel, unbeknownst to Charles, had managed to prepare an old-school picnic basket, and not far from the bank was an old wooden picnic table.

"I think so," Ethel said with a big grandmotherly smile.

Charles, Davy, and Kenny made their way to the table and sat down while Claude and Ethel laid out a red-and-white checkered cloth and set out the contents of the basket. There was fried chicken, mashed potatoes, green beans, macaroni and cheese, biscuits, and an apple pie. To wash it all down, there was a pitcher of lemonade. Charles laughed at the thought of all that being in the basket Ethel was carrying. What a spread!

"This looks so good. I'm going to eat all of it," Kenny said.

"Not before we say the blessing," Ethel said with a finger pointed to Kenny, who had already grabbed a biscuit and had it halfway to his mouth.

"Yes, ma'am," Kenny said as he set the biscuit down in front of him.

"Claude, why don't you bless the food for us," Ethel said.

"Let's pray," Claude said as he bowed his head and closed his eyes. Everyone at the table followed suit. Then Claude cleared his throat and began. "Dear God, we thank You for this food. We thank You for the ability to be able to enjoy it with friends. Help us as we seek to serve and honor You until the very end. In Jesus' name we pray, amen."

Everyone began to fix their plates and drinks. After a moment Charles looked over at Kenny, who was thoroughly enjoying the meal. "How is it, Kenny?"

"So good," Kenny said with a mouthful of food.

Ethel turned her head to the boy. "No talking with food in your mouth, darling."

"Yes, ma'am, Kenny said, without even realizing that he was once again speaking with a mouthful of food.' Ethel started to say something, but Claude elbowed her lightly so she kept her mouth shut.

"As always, your food is top notch, Ethel," Davy complemented.

"Thank you," Ethel replied. "I love to cook for others. Eating with others is a special thing. It makes me think of all those great meals I had with my family growing up."

Charles noticed out of the corner of his eye that Kenny had put his fork down and pushed his plate back. He seemed deep in thought. Kenny had said he was sent here for Charles, but he couldn't help wondering if he was supposed to initiate the conversation first. God had obviously brought Kenny here for a reason.

"Kenny, is there anything you'd like to talk about?" Charles asked.

"You want to talk about Jesus don't you?" Kenny replied.

CHAPTER 23

Somehow, this situation felt very different from the other two conversations he'd had with Tristan and Kayla. There was a sense of confusion and nervousness in Charles that surprised him. The more he thought about it, the less he felt like Kenny needed him in the way Kayla and Tristan had. But he still wanted to try to help Kenny. Maybe that was just his desire to feel like he had some control in the situation. "If you'd like to talk about Jesus, I'm all ears."

"You're not sure if I know Jesus, right?" Kenny replied. "But I do. He's my friend. He loves me."

Charles appreciated Kenny's firmness in his comments. In fact, it left him at a loss for words. Thankfully, Charles wasn't alone in this conversation.

"So you've asked for forgiveness of your sins and asked to receive what Jesus did on the cross for you?" Davy asked in a gentle way that one typically speaks to small children on such delicate topics.

"Yes, sir," Kenny said. "I get to see Him soon, but first I had to come and see you guys."

The directness of Kenny's comments made everyone in the group look at each other in quiet recognition of what this place was. Charles had assumed that Claude and Ethel were aware that this was not the same Bayou Refuge where they had lived for so many years, but some other place entirely. Davy put his head down as if he were contemplating what he could say in response to that statement. There was something very heartbreaking about a child acknowledging his own mortality. Something that, the previous evening, a grown-up was unable to do.

"I like it here. I get out of that chair and can talk. I can't really do that stuff at home. I just sleep a lot," Kenny continued, looking directly at Charles. The man in white in my room told me that I had to come here and make you smile. He said you were having a bad day and had important work to do, and my job was important too. He said I had to make you smile and then tell you that it's not your job to make people do anything. It's only your job to love them and point them to Jesus."

Davy looked up at Charles. "Seems like a good thing to remember. Their job is to *decide*; our job is to *share*."

Ethel, who was sitting next to Kenny, put her arm around his shoulder and hugged him like a grandmother hugging a grandchild who had made her proud. "You did such a good job of passing that message along. You're such a wise little boy."

Kenny leaned into the hug and rested against Ethel's side. He closed his eyes as if taking in the moment, savoring the comfort and peace of being here with these people. After a moment, he looked up at Charles and broke the silence. "What's it like?"

"What do you mean?" Charles asked. "What's what like?"

"What's it like when you leave this place and go over to Jesus?" Kenny asked. "I'm not scared. I'm just wondering."

Tears came into Charles's eyes, and he fought as much as he could to not let them fall. Here was a young boy, one who would never get to live a life like he had, like his son had, like any of these people at this table had. He was already faced with the reality of eternity. Part of it didn't seem fair. However, being in this place and seeing God's hand in everything, then contemplating what eternity would be like . . . Well, anyone in their right mind would want to be with Christ when faced with living in a sinful, fallen world or the peace of God. Like the words of the Apostle Paul in Philippians 1:21, "To live is Christ and to die is gain."

"I don't know, Kenny," Charles said. "I can tell you what I think based on God's Word. Scripture says that being absent from the body means to be present with the Lord. So I imagine that this old world will fade in your eyes, like it's disappearing, then you'll open your eyes and be in the most beautiful place you could ever imagine. As pretty as the bayou is, it will be prettier. Mountains bigger than you could imagine, oceans deeper, buildings built to perfection, glorious animals that we've never laid eyes on, people and angels walking with you and bringing you to Jesus, who I would imagine would give you the best hug you've ever gotten."

"Even better than Mrs. Ethel's hugs?" Kenny asked. His seriousness on a topic like this could only be present in a small child.

"Yes, dear," Ethel replied. "Even better than mine."

"You'll be able to run and play and have all the energy you could imagine. No need to rest in a chair. You'll be able to say whatever you want to Jesus without any trouble. Your voice, your body, simply everything is going to work just fine," Davy said.

"And you guys will be there too?" Kenny asked.

"Yeah, I reckon sooner or later we'll be there too," Claude commented.

The group sat in silence for a few moments, each thinking about eternity and praying for Kenny in their hearts, torn between the sadness of this little one nearing the end but rejoicing in the hope that he had. The wind blew through the fog, and a cool breeze swept over them in a soft reassuring way, as if God was reminding them that He was there with them in that moment. After a while Kenny began to throw his ball up against a tree and let it bounce back to him. He would try to catch it but missed it most of the time. However, he was quite amused by his little game as were the others. They watched the little boy run and play. He seemed comforted by the conversation, and he had certainly comforted and encouraged them. Charles had felt encouraged, and the pain from the previous evening's conversation with Kayla began to slip away.

"How about some of that pie?" Claude interjected after several minutes. Everyone seemed excited about the idea, and Ethel began to cut everyone a slice and set it in front of them. However, when she turned to ask Kenny if he wanted to come back to the table and get a slice, she noticed that he wasn't there. The group all glanced around, looking for the little boy but seeing him nowhere.

"Kenny, you need to come and get some of this pie before I eat it all," Charles said loudly.

"Where are you, Kenny?" Ethel shouted.

"Dear, I think . . ." Claude said.

"Oh, you do?" Ethel asked.

"I do," Claude replied.

"Amen," Davy added. "We'll see him soon."

CHAPTER 24

No one ended up eating the pie. They just sat there and tried to make small talk for a few minutes before Charles excused himself and decided to head back to his room. Davy followed behind him. It didn't surprise Charles. He figured Davy would want to make sure he was okay. And as strange as everything was around him, he didn't mind having someone check on him.

"Tomorrow," Davy said as the two men walked.

"The last conversation?" Charles asked.

"Yeah, one more," Davy clarified.

"What about Kenny? Why didn't you count him? I mean, I get that he did more to help me than I did to help him. But still, why couldn't you tell me that was coming? He practically scared the living daylights out of me when he showed up in my room this morning," Charles said, unable to hold in the question that had been rolling around in his brain.

Davy smiled slightly and looked off to the side for a second as he tried to gather his thoughts. "I didn't know you'd be interacting with Kenny like that. I'd seen the little fellow playing around here. Of course he wasn't the only one. I was certain there'd be three. I'm not sure how Kenny fits into all of this, but I know as sure as I'm standing here that he wasn't part of that three."

"How do you know?" Charles asked, wanting to get some insight into what was happening and how all of this worked.

Davy stopped walking and tilted his head. "I honestly don't know. Sometimes in my mind I'm convinced that someone has told me something, and I remember having conversations with people, talking with them on my phone at the office or being convinced we had talked at a meeting in a coffee shop or restaurant recently. And other times it feels like I just know with a level of certainty that is unquestionable."

"Sorry," Charles replied. "I don't mean to be a pest. I'm just trying to figure out how all of this works. But truth be told, there's probably no way that my mind could comprehend it anyway."

"That's how I feel," Davy said. "Except I tell myself that when I get to the other side it's all going to make more sense."

Charles liked that thought because it appealed to the side of him that wanted control. The idea that soon everything would make sense. He was assuming that once he had his last conversation, it would be his turn to leave. He felt like Kenny, wondering what would happen. He couldn't help but ask his friend and mentor what his thoughts were. "Davy, what do you think is going to happen after my last conversation?"

"Are you scared?" Davy asked with compassion in his voice.

"Probably more nervous than scared about the uncertainty and finality of it all, I guess."

The two began walking again. Charles waited while Davy gathered his thoughts. After several moments, the older man spoke. "I don't fully know. Not sure if you pass on, if you wake back up with your family, or if you get transported to some other place where God wants you to do something else. I wish I knew."

"No certainty," Charles said, laughing a little.

"No, I guess not," Davy said. "But I do know this."

"What's that?"

"We walk by faith. Faith in the one who made us, who sent His Son to save us, and who has a plan for us even when we can't see it. You and I have walked through faith in some tough ministry situations. You know as well as I do that church is not always the nicest place. But by faith in God we trusted and have endured. We just need to do it a little longer. God's been so good to let me be useful again. I don't really care where He has me, but at this time I'm blessed to have you with me."

Charles thought about faith. At its simplest form, faith is trust. There had been moments in his life where it took all he had to trust God. It wasn't a natural reaction but a willing choice and a struggle. What Charles found himself struggling with now was the unknown. What exactly was going to happen? How was it going to happen? And what would the struggle would be like for his family? But it came back to trust again. Did he trust God? Was he going to continue trusting God? In his heart he knew he could, but it was going to take all that he had. He took a deep breath and tried to calm himself. Then he looked over at his mentor and friend and couldn't help but smile.

"Davy, I'm blessed to have you here with me as well," Charles said.

As the two men approached the lodge where Charles's room was, they told each other goodnight and Charles began to walk inside. As he did, he turned to take one more look at his old friend, who seemed to disappear into the fog. Charles then opened the door and went inside. Walking down the worn, brown-carpeted hallway, he heard a noise, a ringing. It took him a second to realize what it was: the phone in his room. He began to run, almost sprinting to the room, praying in his heart that this was a chance to talk to his wife and children. He threw open the door and nearly tripped when he walked inside. He flipped the lights on and ran to the phone. It had rung only a few seconds earlier, but he feared that the call was not going to come through. He picked up the phone and put it to his ear.

"Hello, I'm here."

Suddenly, he wasn't in the room anymore. He couldn't figure out where he was, but he recognized a voice.

"Come on, Charles. I saw you stirring." It was his wife. All of the sudden Charles could feel himself lying on a bed. He tried to move but couldn't. It felt like there were things stuck in his arm. Even though he couldn't open his eyes to see Deborah, he could feel her soft hand holding his. He could hear the beep of a machine, a steady rhythm. It was almost soothing.

"Open those eyes up. See the world again," Deborah encouraged. "Everyone is praying for you and waiting for you."

Charles tried to open his eyes with everything he had. He pushed with as much energy and thought as he could, giving all of his focus to trying to open his eyes. Still nothing. Then he figured maybe just opening one eye would be better. Perhaps that would be easier. So he picked his right eye. He asked God for strength just to see Deborah's face for one second. To see her one more time. He exerted all the focus and strength he had, and for just a second he thought it opened just a little, and a burst of light came in, but then he couldn't make it move. He was so close, but it wasn't going to happen. Feeling her hand over his, he began to try to move it even just a little to reassure her. With a lot of effort, he could feel his pointer finger move up slightly. So little, in fact, that when he did it the first time, she didn't notice. However, when she did it a second time, he heard her voice again.

"I knew you were still there. You got some fight left in you yet. You're going to open those eyes soon. I know it."

Then it was over. Charles was back in the room at Bayou Refuge, sitting at the desk with the receiver up to his ear. He couldn't hear anything except the beeping and the noise of a machine. He hung up the phone and suddenly became aware of how tired he was, much like the day he arrived here.

It took all his strength to move from the chair to the bed, but somehow he mustered the energy. And without even turning the lights off, he fell into a deep sleep.

CHAPTER 25

Charles dreamed of his family that night. It all blurred together, flowing from one scene of his life to another, as well as moments he hadn't experienced yet but hoped to. In one dream he was there with Connor, throwing a baseball back and forth in the backyard when Connor wasn't much older than Kenny had been. Connor was asking questions about God. Charles remembered this moment. It wasn't long after this that Connor had given his life to Christ and was baptized. Connor seemed to feel comfortable asking questions while throwing the baseball. He'd say, "How come I've never seen an angel?" or "Why did Uncle Carl have to die?" Charles would try to answer the question as best as he could. Then they would throw the ball in silence for a few minutes until Connor asked another question. Charles loved having spiritual conversations, and having them with his son was a far richer experience than he'd ever imagined.

In another scene he was with Shelby. They were sitting at the kitchen table, working on a science project. She was building a solar system. Even though she was only eight at the time she was so focused and serious that Charles realized he wasn't really needed, so he just sat back and watched as she painted the balls that represented the planets. He loved her seriousness but also liked to make her smile.

"Dad, hand me Mercury," Shelby asked as she was preparing to put the different planets on little stands that she had made.

Charles handed her Jupiter and waited to see what her response would be. "Dad, this is Jupiter. I need Mercury. It's yellow and red, and little." Charles then handed her the sun. She was trying to adjust the stand and reached to grab what she expected to be the small planet without looking at it. When she felt something large, she gave her dad a side glance. Recognizing even at the age of eight that the sense of humor of a dad can be lame at times.

"What?" Charles asked, faking seriousness. "I'm just trying to help."

"Did you ever study the solar system?" Shelby asked, half joking. "Because I'm starting to wonder."

He handed her Mercury and then, when she requested, Venus. She silently attached the planets, but when she asked for Earth, he handed her Mars. Without ever looking at him, she acted like she was about to put it on a stand. But before the Styrofoam ball touched it, she tossed it back at Charles and hit him square in the forehead. She burst out in laughter as Charles picked up Pluto and with a light toss hit her shoulder. It was a perfect moment that showed both her intelligence and her sweet spirit.

Then he found himself in front of a pond with a fishing pole next to his dad and grandpa. He was wearing a faded collared shirt and old blue jeans. He was eleven. He knew this because his grandpa died when he was twelve, and this was one of the last memories he had with his grandpa before he began to get sick. He was holding a rod and reel that had a line in the water. He could hear both of the men talking.

His dad, a man with broad shoulders and large arms, was wearing a pair of blue jeans and a worn red T-shirt. "You aren't going to catch a bass on that lure, Dad. Not here," Charles's dad said to his grandpa.

His grandpa, whom he called Pops, was wearing a faded pair of khakis and a short-sleeve red-and-blue button-up shirt. "Yeah, you will. Just give it a minute. Pop that line a little, Charles."

Charles gave the line a pop as he reeled it in slowly. He waited several seconds and then did it again. He repeated this for a while and began to think like his dad. This was a hopeless endeavor. Then something changed quickly. The line went tight, and the fish was running off with it, moving so quick that Charles's dad thought he was going to lose the old rod and reel. As they began to pull and reel, the pole bent down, exposing previous cracks and strains that had accumulated over the years, and Charles thought the pole might break.

"Come on! Pull it in," his dad said.

His grandpa began to laugh. A few seconds later the fish stopped struggling and broke the surface of the water and revealed itself to be a large bass. Charles pulled it onto shore while his dad shot his grandpa a humorous look.

Pops just smiled and said, "The old man still has it."

Charles suddenly saw himself somewhere he had never been before. He could tell it was an old country church just by the décor and style. He was standing in a room with tan carpet, wood-panel walls, and pictures of maps of Israel and Bible verses. It must have been a Sunday school room. He heard a door open and turned to see a woman enter the room in a wedding dress. The long white dress sparkled and flowed down to the ground. The woman turned to face Charles. There was something familiar and not right about her at the same time. He recognized her face, the way her whole face smiled . . . but this couldn't be.

"Daddy, how do I look?" Charles realized in this moment that the young woman in front of him was in fact Shelby. The breath left his body as he stared in amazement at how beautiful his daughter looked. "Does the dress look all right?"

"Darling, you look absolutely beautiful," Charles said as he tried to hold back a tear from falling but failed miserably.

"Aw, Dad, don't cry. You'll have me crying and messing up all this makeup," Shelby said as she turned to avoid looking at him.

"Give me a minute. I'll be okay," he said..

Then he heard a knock on the door behind him. "It's about to start," someone said.

"You ready to walk your little girl down the aisle?" Shelby asked playfully.

"He better take good care of you."

"Dad, you know he will. He's a good man, and I think he's getting to be a pretty good preacher too."

The thought of his daughter marrying a preacher made his heart happy and full. As he was basking in this thought, the door opened. A woman was standing there, motioning for the two of them to come out.

Once he walked out of the door, he found himself somewhere else. He was walking with Deborah down the hallway of a hospital. The floors had bright-white tile; the walls were grey sheetrock with a wooden bar hanging off the wall. Brown wooden doors with numbers and pictures of storks and teddy bears filled the hallway. Hand sanitizer dispensers hung just to the side of each door. Deborah looked a little older, with a few more greys in her hair. She elbowed him to stop. "This is the room. Grab some of that sanitizer now. We don't want to bring in any germs." The two of them cleaned their hands, and she led him into a room. He saw a clear plastic crib on a cart with an empty blue blanket in it. A large open window let rays of sunlight into the room. In the middle of the room up against the wall was a hospital bed with a young woman lying in it with her arm resting on the leg of a young man in blue jeans and a grey polo holding a baby wrapped in a blanket.

"Hey, grandpa," the woman said as she looked at Charles. He looked over to the young man again and recognized him as his son several years down the road. The same haircut, a little longer than he'd like, but somehow it fit Connor. And the baby on his lap had to be his grandson.

"Hey, Dad, you want to hold Jacob?" Charles looked down at the little baby, a precious child that was cooing and looking right at Charles.

"Deborah, do you want to?" Charles asked.

"Oh no! The deal was if it was a granddaughter, I got to hold her first. If he was a grandson, you got to hold the baby first. And since we've already got two granddaughters, I think it's your turn to hold one first," Deborah said.

"Two granddaughters?" Charles said, smiling. "We're so blessed. Where are the girls?"

"Shelby has them," Connor replied. "But they should be up here in a little while."

"And Shelby doesn't have much longer until hers gets here," Kara, Connor's wife, added.

Charles couldn't believe it: four grandchildren! Once again, his heart filled with joy. Even though he was seeing everything so quickly, it was somehow as if the fullness of the experience wasn't diminished. He held the baby in his arms and smiled at him. "Hey, Jacob! I'm so glad to meet you." Charles knew that babies smiling at this age doesn't mean much. However, when Jacob smiled, Charles was going to believe that it was intentional and just for him.

Deborah, Connor, and Kara visited about how labor went, brands of diapers, how to help the baby sleep, and all sorts of other things. Charles added a comment or two in here or there but was contented simply holding this little baby.

A while later the door opened to reveal a very pregnant Shelby, Colby, and two little twin girls, Sara and Sonya. Charles handed Jacob over to Deborah and, as if right on cue, the two girls, no more than three or four, ran over and wrapped their arms around him. Then the room went white.

Charles was now lying in a hospital bed. At first, he thought he had woken up. He could smell Deborah's perfume, and there was an old episode of a television show he liked watching. However, he noticed he didn't have any cords or equipment hooked up to him. He turned and saw Deborah seated in a chair, working on a crossword puzzle, but she was much older, with a head full of white hair. Somehow, though, she was as beautiful as ever. He looked down at his hands and saw how wrinkled and shaky they were and realized he must be older now too. Seeing him stir, Deborah put her crossword book down and stood up very slowly, working through her aches and pains, and walked over to Charles.

"How are you feeling, dear?" she asked.

He had to think about that question. He seemed to be tired and achy, knowing somehow that he was dying, but at the same time his heart was at total peace. As Charles tried to turn to her, he noticed that he couldn't move very quickly. He opened his mouth to speak but struggled to say much. His mouth was very dry.

"I'm thirsty," he said. "Can I get some water?"

Deborah picked up a pink plastic cup with a straw in it and brought it up to Charles's mouth after pushing a button to raise the bed and sit him up a bit. He sucked on the straw and found the task to be much harder than he'd expected. However, after a moment cool water came into his mouth and made its way down his throat. He nodded his head after a few seconds to let her know he was done.

"I'm okay," Charles said.

"Well, the kids just left. They all wanted you to get your rest. They love you. Shelby brought you some more of those peach fruit cups you like," Deborah said.

"Is this the end?" Charles asked.

She hesitated for a moment, not knowing how to respond, wanting to make sure that she used the right words. "The doctors said that at your age, they can't do another heart surgery. They figure you'll have another episode sooner rather than later, and it'll probably take you."

"That's okay. If it's my time, I'm ready."

"God's been good to us," Deborah said. The two sat in silence for a few moments, and all Charles could think about were the things he had experienced in his life and the things he had just seen. Even though he hadn't really lived all of this life, it felt like he had. It was a rich blessing from God that he didn't expect.

"Yes, He is," Charles said. "I'm ready when the Lord's ready.

CHAPTER 26

"I'm ready when the Lord's ready," Charles heard himself saying. He repeated it again, "I'm ready when the Lord's ready."

He opened his eyes and found his room bright with light. It felt as if the fog had lifted some, and sunlight was shining into his room. Charles thought about the dream and those precious memories he got to relive. Seeing his father and grandfather was so powerful. Being back in favorite memories with his children also warmed his heart. However, seeing into a possible future was hard to understand. The only thing he could think of was that perhaps God let Charles get a taste of those moments in that way because he wasn't going to get to experience those events with his family. It was hard to process, but there was a sense of peace now in his heart. If that was what the Lord wanted, he was okay with it.

He got up slowly and made his way to the window. While the fog was still surrounding the camp, it seemed like it had lit up even a little more than the previous day, and a bit more light was shining through. His spirit lifted. Not in a way that made him feel like his problems were gone, but more like knowing that in whatever he faced, God was going to walk with him through it. Perhaps today was the day of the last conversation he'd have. Something made him want to dress up for it. He went over to the closet in the room where he had hung up the khaki pants and dress shirt and decided to dress nice for the day. He washed his face, shaved with a razor and shaving cream he found in the bathroom, and fixed his hair. As he did, he thought about who he might be visiting with today.

He recalled his conversations with Tristan and Kayla. He had been overjoyed by his conversation with Tristan, even though at first it seemed like the young man wasn't going to give His life to Christ. Then, at the last possible moment, he did. His conversation with Kayla had broken his heart. Just when he thought that she was allowing God to get through to her, she walked out of that door. The thought still hurt him deep in his heart. Charles redirected his thoughts to prayer and asked God to prepare his own heart, to give him the right words, and to prepare the heart of the person he was going to be seeing soon.

Charles stood in the mirror and examined himself, making sure that he looked appropriate for a pastor. Charles knew that ultimately God didn't care about the external, but he had been brought up old school and actually liked dressing up. In his mind, it made him ready for whatever he'd face as a pastor, whether the day held hospital visits, meetings with committees, or drop-in office visits to talk about the gospel or other spiritual matters. He put a stray hair back in place and gave himself a slight smile as he thought about part of his daily routine. Charles would often ask Deborah if he looked okay before he left. Sometimes, if she was in the kitchen or reading a book, Deborah wouldn't even lift up her head or turn her head to look at him. She'd just say, "You look great today, dear."

"How do you know? You're not even looking," he'd reply.

Then he'd hear the always encouraging but not very helpful, "You always look good to me dear."

It was funny how God used conversations like that to help get him ready for the day. When the kids were little, he'd hardly be able to get out the door if he'd forgotten to hug them. Sometimes when they were little, Shelby or Connor would beg to go to work with him. It always broke his heart and made him smile at the same time.

Charles made his way over to the welcome center where he and Davy had enjoyed coffee and biscuits that first day. The brightness of the day was welcoming. He could feel the warmth of the sun on him, breaking its way through the fog. However, he wasn't sure if he really was feeling it, or if the fog had lifted at all, or if was just his mind playing some sort of trick on him. As he walked, the damp grass stuck to his black shoes, but he tried to not let that upset him. He saw Claude walking near the house and waved, but Claude didn't return the gesture. It seemed like he was in the middle of some task. Maybe he was looking for something.

Charles came into the welcome center, greeted by the smell the coffee, and saw Davy, who was dressed in the same khakis red collared shirt he had been wearing the previous day. He was sitting on the old couch sipping on a cup of coffee in a Bayou Refuge mug, looking at the pictures on the wall. Charles walked over to the table where the coffee was and poured himself some in a black mug with Psalm 42:1 printed in white lettering.

"No biscuits today?" Charles asked as he headed to a cushioned chair across from the couch and sat down.

"No, had to make the coffee myself too. Hadn't done that in a while."

"Oh no," Charles replied with a slight laugh. "So if it's not good I know who to blame it on."

"Like riding a bike, my boy. Learned it in the Army, and haven't lost that skill," Davy said, chuckling. "I guess Ethel got tied up with fixing lunch."

"Third guest arriving today?"

"Yeah, should be getting here shortly. His name is Martin."

"I'm looking forward to it—the last one."

"This one is going to be different," Davy said with his voice taking a slightly more serious tone.

"How so?"

"Martin is a very religious man, and you know as well as I do that religion has kept a lot of people from really knowing Jesus."

"Hmm," Charles replied as he thought about conversations he'd had over the years with people who knew a lot about God but didn't really *know* Him.

"The greatest enemies Jesus faced were the religious leaders of His day. You know as well as I do that the hardest challenges in most churches are often from the people who consider themselves to be the most religious."

The two sat in silence for a moment, sipping on their coffee. Charles saw Davy turn his head down and look at the floor. Something seemed off, as if something else was bothering him.

"You okay, Davy?" Charles asked.

Davy hesitated for a moment, then looked up at Charles. He sat his coffee cup on the old coffee table, then after a few seconds answered. "I've been spending more time here."

"What do you mean?" Charles asked. He knew that Davy came and went from this place.

"When I'm home, I'm so confused. I don't always know where I am, but I know my Martha. I've always joked that I'm lost without her. But when I'm home, I am lost without her. She and Jesus are all I really know when I'm there. I can't even figure out how to get my fingers to button up a shirt or my hands to put a fork of food to my mouth. Sometimes I don't even know that she's my wife, but I still know her on a deep level. It makes sense in my heart that she's there with me. But things have been different lately. It used to feel like I'd show up here a few times a week, then it became a time or two a day, just for a while, like I had something I needed to do. But lately . . ." Davy he turned his eyes back to the pictures on the wall.

"Davy, I guess as things go, the nature of the—" Charles stopped himself.

"Spit it out, boy," Davy said a little bit agitated, the military directness in him surfacing. "We're both men here, so let's not pull punches."

"Pull punches," Charles said with a slight laugh. "Who didn't tell me that I was on the edge of death in some altered spiritual state of existence, or whatever this place is?"

"Fair enough," Davy replied, relaxing a little and smiling at Charles. "But you got to admit that may not be something you just want to drop on someone. You would have lost your mind if I immediately said, 'Oh, by the way, you're hooked up on life support right now. You're probably not going to see your family again. But God's put it in my heart that you need to talk to some people.'"

"I hear ya," Charles agreed.

"But there's no more cats in the bag, son," Davy said. "Death is the great equalizer, and best I can figure we're running toward it in a full sprint, trying to figure out what in the world is happening along the way because there's not a manual for this place. So just say what you think."

Charles gathered his thoughts for a second. "I've been thinking about the nature of your disease and this place. I think that when you have moments when you lose touch with reality, God brings you here. Early in the disease your mind isn't leaving as much. You're more aware of what's going on around you even if it's still confusing. But when you mentally check out, you come here. So what I think is that as the disease progresses, you're coming here more."

"That's what I was afraid of," Davy replied. "As bad as the disease is, I guess it is hardwired in us to hold on as long as we can. It's just hard being away from Martha so much. But you know, if I had to go through this with someone other than my bride or my family, I'm glad it's you, Charles. Whatever this is, I'm glad to be here with a friend. Still, it's hard sometimes. I can feel my temper welling up, wanting to be back home and getting angry at God." Davy lowered his head and processed his thoughts for a minute. "I don't want to go back to that place of anger and hurting others, but I just miss her."

"When I rest here, I dream of my family, and they are the most vivid dreams, like I'm right there with them," Charles said, trying to offer some sort of encouragement. "I know it's not the same, but it sure makes my heart feel better, like a gift from God. Last night I saw . . ."

Charles couldn't get the words out, and tears began to fall. Davy looked at his friend and offered the softest of grins. "Now it's your turn to get choked up, I guess." Davy said, rubbing a tear from his left eye.

Charles laughed a little and then gathered his composure. "Davy, I saw my little girl grown, walking down the aisle. I saw my grandkids, and it felt like I was there. It felt like I had all of the memories as if I had lived a full life. I may not actually get those things, but God in His mercy has somehow made that okay in my heart."

The two sat in silence for a moment, processing everything. Charles had a desire to stretch his legs and step outside. He looked over at Davy, who at this point had picked up his cup of coffee and was sipping on it. "Davy, I think I'm going to step outside for a moment."

Charles opened the wooden doors and walked out onto the dirt parking lot in front of the welcome center. He noticed his own car parked there and for a moment felt an almost overwhelming desire to hop in the car and drive off, head back home and hug his wife and kids. He smiled at the thought but shook it off, knowing that dwelling on it wouldn't do him any good. Charles paced for a moment in front of the building, praying in his heart for God to help him focus on the conversations he'd be having with Martin. It was then he saw a upscale black sedan pull up, no doubt an older model but one that had been well-kept. He watched the car pull up next to his and then stop.

The driver was a large, well-dressed, bald Black man, and it made Charles wish he'd had a suit with him. He got out of the car wearing a blue suit, holding an expensive leather overnight bag. He stepped to the back door of the vehicle and grabbed a hanging bag, probably with another suit and some dress shirts if Charles had to guess. Once he had everything, he turned to Charles with a big grin. "Hello, my friend! It's nice to see you today. Despite this fog, I know one thing: God is good."

"Yes, He is," Charles replied, taken aback by the guest for some reason that he couldn't express. "You must be Martin. I'm Charles. Why don't you come on in? Can I help you with your bags?"

"No, I think I'm good," he said. "Nice to meet you, Charles."

"Would you like a cup of coffee?" Charles asked as they entered into the building.

"You know, I'm feeling a bit off this morning. I think I would like a cup."

"Set your bags down on this table over here," Charles said, pointing to a table by the door. "I'll fix you a cup. Do you take cream and sugar?"

"Yes, I do," Martin answered with a slight laugh. "Load it up."

"Absolutely," Charles said as Martin set his bags down and walked over to the couch and took a seat.

Charles looked around for Davy, but he was nowhere to be found. He knew he'd probably stepped out the back door, but he sure was hoping that maybe he had slipped back home for a while. Then Charles turned back and looked at Martin, who was getting himself situated in his seat. Charles couldn't shake the strange feeling he had when he looked at Martin. Then it dawned on him; he knew who Martin was.

CHAPTER 27

As he fixed the coffee and brought it to Martin, he tried to figure out where he had seen the man before. He was certainly dressed in such a way that indicated that he was financially well-off. The nice black sedan also spoke to that as well. Something about his facial features seemed very recognizable, but in a way that indicated he had seen Martin's picture or face on something at some point.

After a few minutes of small talk, much in the same way that Kayla had, Martin seemed really exhausted and asked if he'd be able to go to his room for a while and sneak in a nap. Charles was glad to let him know that was a good idea. He remembered how tired he had been when he got here. He thought back to the truth Davy had shared with him long ago: sometimes the most spiritual thing you can do is take a nap. A little rest was good for the soul and the body.

Charles felt wide awake, though, and the thought occurred to him that perhaps he ought to make his way to the little white house where Ethel and Claude lived and check on them and the status of the upcoming meal. It was unlike Ethel to not be prepared and for coffee to not be ready in the welcome center. Something must not be right. He tried not to think about it too much. Perhaps in the business of everything over the past few days, it had slipped Ethel's mind and was nothing of major concern.

The damp grass and dirt stuck to his shoes again as he walked toward the cabin, and the fog made his dress shirt and pants stick to him, making him feel a bit silly for dressing so nicely. Especially considering that dressing up in this altered state of reality didn't matter quite like it had in the world he no longer could be a part of and see. Still, as well-dressed as Martin had been upon arrival, it seemed like this was something that would matter to him, so he had to be willing to endure wearing dress clothes here. As he approached the raised porch, he could see Claude leaning on it and scanning the grounds of Bayou Refuge as if he was still looking for something.

"Everything okay, Claude?" Charles asked.

"I don't know," Claude said without looking up. Clearly, the man viewed something as very wrong. "I can't find Ethel. I've walked this whole place twice, checked every building, and I can't find her anywhere."

"I noticed that coffee wasn't made this morning in the welcome center, so I wondered if she was okay. It's not like her to leave something undone. She's quite the perfectionist," Charles said, then questioned if his words had helped or worsened the situation.

"She likes to make sure everything is set so we're good hosts. She's always been that way," Claude said. "I like it though. It has always kept me focused on serving God. I'm no good at this stuff on my own."

Claude let out a slight laugh with his last statement. Charles thought that perhaps the laugh was intended to keep him from crying. "Has this ever happened before?" Charles asked.

Claude thought to himself for a moment before responding. The elderly man's forehead crinkled a little bit as if an unpleasant thought had come to mind. "Early on when we came back here, we'd come and go, and sometimes we'd miss each other—like we couldn't figure out where the other had gone. But that hasn't happened in a long time. We haven't left here since I don't know when."

"What do we do?" Charles asked, surprised by the confusion in his own voice.

"We go on," Claude said, his voice slightly cracking but portraying a new sense of confidence. "There's a sandwich tray and a pot of soup as well as a pie and some tea in the fridge here. That man is here, needing one last spiritual conversation. We need to give it to him and trust God to take care of Ethel."

Moving on felt a bit wrong in Charles's mind, although he knew Claude was right. All the two men could do was pray and carry on. Praying seemed right in the moment. "Claude, can we pray together?"

"I'd like that," the old man replied.

Charles walked over to Claude, put a hand on the man's shoulder, and they bowed their heads. "Dear heavenly Father . . ."

CHAPTER 28

Charles and Claude had set the sandwich tray and soup in the café. The sandwiches looked fancy, like something you'd get at a catered event. They were on some sort of special wheat bread with a thin slice of turkey, tomato, lettuce, and spicy mayonnaise. The soup was roasted red pepper, and the pie was blueberry. When they arrived at the café, Claude remembered that there were some small bags of potato chips. He set a few on the table next to the warmer containing the soup and the tray of sandwiches. Thankfully, some sweet tea was left over from the meal with Kayla, and he set that out as well as a small ice bucket.

Charles's instinct was to make conversation by asking where the soup and sandwiches had come from. However, Charles knew that Claude had no idea. He had probably found them in the fridge when he woke up that morning. There was no point in asking a question like that now. God's provision, although just as real in the world where he was fighting for his life, was more obvious in many ways here.

"Everything look okay?" Claude asked.

"Yeah, it looks good, Claude," Charles said. "Thank you for helping set it up."

I'm gonna head back to the house if that's all right, maybe she's there waiting for me," Claude said.

"Sure," Charles replied. Then he watched the elderly man walk slowly out of the café, looking like a child who couldn't find his best friend.

Charles waited for a few moments in one of the chairs. His mind wondered to what might have happened to Martin to bring him to this place and if he'd be more like Tristan, who knew he was nearing the end of his life, or more like Kayla and not have a clue. However, he didn't get to explore those thoughts for long because it seemed that within a few minutes of Claude leaving, Martin made his way into the café. He was wearing the same blue suit and white shoes. He seemed a bit more chipper. It was evident that he had gotten some rest.

"I have not slept that well in ages," Martin said.

"I'm glad you could rest, I know a little nap can go a long way to making someone feel ready for whatever comes their way," Charles said, then motioned toward the food table. "Help yourself to some sandwiches. We've also got some soup, chips, and pie."

Martin looked at the table of food and then at Charles, and a big grin swept across his face. "No way! These are all my favorites. God is good! It's going to be a good day."

It seemed that all the meals were foods dear to the guests. Tristan pigged out on the pot roast. Kayla thought the gumbo tasted just like her grandmother's. And now Martin expressed that these simple foods, which had been unnoticed in the fridge, were Martin's favorites. This was something Charles realized could only be orchestrated by God, considering that no one knew the guests coming well enough to pull that off. Martin worked his way through the line fixing portions of each item. Charles did the same even though he didn't have much of an appetite. He had to admit, though, the smell of the soup was almost irresistible. It hit a savory and sweet note that made his mouth water a bit. The two men sat down at the table with their food and glasses of sweet tea.

"May I ask the blessing?" Martin asked.

"Absolutely," Charles replied, a bit caught off guard.

"Dear God, we thank You for this food and this opportunity to be able to eat together as brothers. Thank You for those who You had prepare it for us. And we ask for Your blessing on them. Thank You for those who are here with us, God, that you would open their hearts and minds to You. We ask You to lead us in all that we do. In Jesus' name we pray, amen." Martin then cleared his throat, grabbed his spoon, and tasted the soup.

Part of Charles wondered if maybe someone had gotten something wrong. Was Martin really a man lost in religion? This prayer sounded genuine, like someone who really knew the Lord. Charles sampled some of the soup and gathered his thoughts. The soup was tasty enough that he allowed himself another spoonful before finally speaking.

"Tell me about yourself, Martin."

"I grew up good. Times were tight, but Mama and Daddy loved us, and we never knew we were struggling to get by. Daddy worked no telling how many jobs at a time. Mama made beans and rice taste like a gourmet meal. Every Sunday we were in the church house. Graduated up there high in my senior class. I was the first one in my family to go to college. I always wanted to run my own business. The grocery store in our community wasn't very good, so I had in my mind to get a degree, learn the business, and come back and make it a reality. I didn't figure I'd get rich, but it would be a good living and a way to give back to the community. My dad was my number-one supporter. He worked in a plant and told me as soon as I opened my store, he'd come and work for his son, keep the place looking good and the shelves stocked." Martin laughed a little at that thought. "That was the kind of man he was. If working for me was how he could support and encourage me, then that's what he'd do."

Martin took a bite of a sandwich and a sip of sweet tea as he relished the memory of his father. Then he wiped his mouth with a napkin and continued. "He had a heart attack right before I finished college. About a week before that he had lined it up for me to work as an assistant manager at a grocery store one town over from where we lived as soon as I graduated. He told them I had been bagging groceries and stocking shelves since high school, and no one could do it like I could. He should have been a salesman. And I did! I took the job, worked all the hours I could get there. I delivered pizzas, sold furniture I found on the side of the road, even fixed up and flipped a house. About three years later I had enough capital that the bank gave me a loan when I talked the current grocery store owner into letting me buy the place."

Then it clicked. Charles knew who Martin was. He temporarily forgot where he was and what the purpose of the conversation was. Charles had seen Martin's face in commercials for grocery stores in New Orleans when he lived there. Martin was a very well-known businessman. Charles couldn't contain his excitement at solving this puzzle. "I know who you are! I shopped at your stores and saw you on TV.

"Is that right!" Martin interjected with a smile. "I hope you were pleased and found what you were looking for when you shopped there. Boy, it's a small world, isn't it? So let me tell you, it all started with that one store, but I think maybe because I wanted to impress my dad and honor him, I kept moving forward and doing more. In the process of running the best store I could, developing the best employees I could, trying the help the community as I was able . . . Well, the community ended up blessed me. I was quite financially stable with one store, so when a grocery store across town decided to close its doors, I bought it, giving us two locations. A year later the grocery one town over where I had worked right after college wanted me to buy them out, so I did. Next thing I know, we were regional, I remember having to stop and count them, at that point I had twenty stores. Then it hit me."

"What's that?" Charles asked.

"I had nothing—no life, no identity apart from the stores. I had been so busy chasing success that it felt like it was all I had. I had an auntie pass away, and I couldn't even break away from my own business to go to the funeral. Mama called me and lit into me. That was a wake-up call. I remembered the people I had gone to church with growing up. They were so happy, full of joy, so I slipped back into church. Of course, if you can't tell, I'm an all-in sort of guy. I wanted what they had, so I started doing what they did, trying to read my Bible, praying, and just living out that faith life." Martin laughed a little, then lifted his hand and yelled, "Hallelujah! Praise the Lord."

Charles thought about how to dig a bit deeper into the man's theology. To see what he really believed. Based on Davy's comments and the fact that Martin was here, maybe he knew about Jesus, but had he really received what Jesus did through His death on the cross and the resurrection? Had he really repented of his sins and placed his full trust in Jesus for salvation? Charles wasn't convinced.

"So when did you give your life to Jesus?" Charles asked.

"Oh, I guess after being at the church for a few weeks, I just decided this was who I was going to be and started changing my life," Martin answered.

"Did you change it, or did God change it?" Charles asked, surprised at the question coming out of his mouth, believing that perhaps the Holy Spirit had given him these words.

Martin sat back in his chair, looking a little offended, but then he looked up and stared at the ceiling for a moment with a look of confusion on his face. "That's certainly an interesting question. I wanted what they had. I wanted Jesus, so I just jumped into what they were doing and started seeking God and following the examples of these godly men."

"Did you have that moment of surrender where you gave your life to Christ and received what He did for you?" Charles asked.

"Oh yeah, I got baptized," Martin replied with a bit of confidence.

"That's great, but did you give your life to Christ and make Him the Lord of it?"

"You sound like Elder Brown. He would ask me those sorts of questions every now and then. He tried to talk me out of being baptized because I couldn't answer that," Martin said with a nervous laugh. "I'm trying to be a good person. I'm trying to go to church. I help my employees. I tell them to come to church and to read their Bibles. I give to the church. I sing songs to God. I pray. I really do try to make Jesus my Lord. I'm wanting it to be enough."

"You remind me of Cornelius," Charles said.

"I think I remember that story," Martin said. "That's the God-fearing man who Peter talked to in the book of Acts."

"That's right," Charles said. "God gave Peter a vision to go see Cornelius, who believed in God and supported the work of Jews in the area. He wanted to know more about Jesus but wasn't aware that Jesus was the Messiah who had died for the sins of the world. So in a way, Cornelius was really close to knowing God and having salvation but not quite there."

"And you think that's me?" Martin asked, his scrunched forehead expressing confusion and a little anger.

"Well, you talk a lot about acting the part," Charles replied. "Like following the men in the church who knew Jesus, getting baptized because you thought you were supposed to. You use the right words, and your prayer earlier was beautiful. But we can't just act the part to be saved. 2 Corinthians 5:17 says that if anyone is in Christ he is a new creation. There's a transformation of the inner man that has occurred."

Martin looked deep in thought. Charles imagined that he was carefully thinking over every word that Charles had spoken. After a few seconds he picked up his fork and slowly took a bite of blueberry pie sitting in front of him. Then he put the fork down and looked at Charles like a businessman contemplating a major business decision would.

"I'm on church committees. I've taught Bible studies. I've done so much to help build God's kingdom. And yet in this moment, you're telling me that I'm not in the kingdom? Am I understanding you correctly?"

Charles hesitated to answer because there was a slight hint of aggression and anger in Martin's statement. However, now wasn't the time to back down. "I'm saying that based on what you've said, that there is something missing there. I know that's hard to hear."

"How can you know someone's heart?" Martin replied. "Who do you think you are?"

"I don't know your heart. I just know the words you're saying," Charles replied.

"I'm a good man," Martin sat up in his chair and declared.

"Romans 3:23 says that none of us are good. We have all fallen short of God's perfect standard. So I'd have to disagree."

"I've worked hard to change my life," Martin added.

"Yeah, but Ephesians 2:8 says that we are saved by grace through faith. In other words, we are saved through believing what Jesus did for us, that He died on the cross and rose from the grave. It's not about what we can do; none of us can do enough," Charles said.

Martin looked at Charles intensely for a moment and then smiled. "I like people being direct with me. I hate it when people beat around the bush. I used to tell my employees at the grocery stores, 'I don't care how bad the situation is, you hiding it from me isn't going to fix it.' You've given me a lot to think about. I need to go back to my room and reflect on this some. I'd like to call my pastor too," Martin said and started to get up. Charles's heartbeat picked up its speed. He knew that waiting was not in Martin's best interest. He knew that ordinarily taking some time to think might be okay, but he wasn't sure that Martin had much time left.

"I don't think you should get up and leave yet. I think we need to talk just a little more," Charles said with a definite sense of urgency in his voice. Martin tilted his head signaling interest and sat down. Then he looked over the plate of food in front of him, one item at a time. Martin's eyes glanced around the room, and he smiled as if he had put the pieces of a puzzle together.

"So this is it, huh?" Martin asked. "I knew something was off."

"What do you mean?" Charles asked, thinking that he knew what was going on but not wanting to put words in Martin's mouth.

"Well, Mama said Daddy had some issues with his stomach. Doctors said if he had gone for some checkups, they probably would have caught it. He never was one for doctor visits. I guess I got that trait from him," Martin replied. "What happens when I walk out of that door?"

"I don't know for sure. There's a lot I don't get about this place. Took me a while to figure out where I was or what was going on, but I think this is some sort of last-chance spot for people to get right with God," Charles explained.

"Hmm, I figured seeing all my favorite foods here from different places on top of struggling to remember why I was coming to this place, then having a vague idea about a church retreat. I think I knew it was a dream or something, but I didn't want to think too hard about it. Ultimately, I hate the idea of not being able to work myself into God's good graces. I've read about God's grace and needing faith, but I have worked my tail off for everything I've ever gotten in life. At the end of the day, I knew that I was missing some pieces, but it's hard to let go of that last bit of self and pride. I'd read verses like the ones you're referencing, and I'd think, *Well, that must apply to someone else.* Or I'd just gloss over them."

"You have to come to God on His terms, through faith and repentance, through receiving the gospel," Charles said.

Then Charles watched Martin bow his head, and the once beautifully spoken man called out to God: "God, I've been wanting to do this my way, and I'm sorry. God, I'm so sorry. I spent years paying no mind to You, then all of a sudden I want to earn my way into Your kingdom. God, I come to You broken. Forgive me of my sins. I receive what Jesus did on the cross. I believe He died for my sins and rose from the grave. I believe that Jesus is the way to you, God. I surrender. I give You my life. I turn from my sins. Thank You, God."

Martin kept his head bowed, and Charles watched as tears fell from his face. Charles's heart filled with a joy that was unexplainable, and he had to fight back his own tears. Martin eventually stood and looked at Charles, who stood as well. "Are you some sort of angel?"

"No!" Charles laughed. "Just some old preacher who wound up here and was told to tell some folks about Jesus one last time. I'm just like you. And just like you, I don't know what's going to happen to me when I walk out that door."

"Can I give you a hug, brother?" Martin asked.

"Of course," Charles replied. The two men hugged tightly like two friends who hadn't seen each other in a long time. Then Martin let go of Charles and looked down at the table.

"You know, I'm ready to go see Jesus or face whatever is on the other side of that door. But you think it'd be okay if we finished this pie first?" Martin asked.

"I think that's a great idea," Charles said, then laughed a little, enjoying that he could put off the uncertainty of the coming moments just a little longer.

CHAPTER 29

Each bite seemed to be smaller and slower than the previous one. It wasn't that Charles was scared to face eternity; it was the uncertainty of the process and the human nature within him to cling onto life as he knew it for as long as he could. Despite the joys of heaven, letting go of life was hard. Martin seemed to be in the same boat, except he didn't eat slowly. He went back for a second slice and then a smaller third slice. Although, based on the way he slowed down on his last piece, Charles assumed he had only grabbed it to buy another minute of time.

"You know, most grocery stores have mass-produced pies and cakes that are frozen and then shipped in the plastic containers," Martin said. Charles knew exactly what he was talking about. He had picked up many of them for church fellowships over the years. Martin finally pushed his pie away and looked at Charles. "I always resented the fact that we sold those. There's nothing like something freshly made. There's some love in the process of fixing it. This here is top-notch! A lady who had a bakery back home would make these. It was always a process to order them, and half the time she'd tell you she had too many orders. I tried to track her down and hire her to come train our bakers. I couldn't find her though. I recruited a few other bakers, and they did okay, but no one ever could come close to this pie right here. This is my favorite meal. What's yours, Charles?"

Charles hadn't much thought about it, but it seemed each of the guests had the food that meant something special to them. He closed his eyes and thought for a moment. "You know, I really like lots of foods: steak and potatoes, or a pizza cooked in a brick oven. I even like a fresh chef salad. But it's always been more about who I'm eating with and the conversation than the food. These conversations right here, this is what makes me happiest."

"Pretty profound," Martin said. Then he stood up and dusted his jacket off and wiped his mouth with a napkin before setting it back on the table. "Is there any point to picking up after ourselves?"

"I'm not sure," Charles said, laughing. "I guess not."

The two men made their way to the door of the café without saying a word. Martin put his hand on the knob and began to turn it. Then he slowly pushed the door open, and Charles could see the fog, the grass, the trees, and the cabins in front of him. He looked at Martin, who was still there and but confused. Charles wasn't sure what he expected to happen, but he definitely expected something. Martin took a deep breath and stepped outside.

"Did you gentlemen have a good visit?" Charles heard from outside the door. The voice initially startled him causing him to jump a bit. However, he recognized quickly that the voice belonged to his friend Davy.

"Yes, we did, brother," Martin replied. "Probably the most important one I'd ever had."

Charles followed Martin out of the door and closed it behind them. He stood outside and saw his friend in his khaki pants wearing the familiar red polo and smiling.

"Good to see you, Davy," Charles said. The two men stood in silence. Martin and Charles no doubt wanting some guidance on what would happen next. Charles felt like based on the nervous smile on Davy's face, he knew something and was supposed to share it. "So what happens now?"

"I think that phone in your room was ringing earlier. Might be good to call home one more time. Then I think it's time for you to head out," Davy replied.

"Head out where?" Charles asked. "And what about Martin?"

Davy looked over at Martin and smiled. "Martin, would you be willing to stay for a while and help me out here? There might be a couple of guests coming in who you could visit with."

"I think I'm supposed to say yes," Martin said with a look of someone trying to solve a puzzle, then a big smile broke out on his face. "I think I'd really like to do that."

"Why don't you head on over to that welcome center?" Davy said. "I'll meet you there in a bit. I need to have a moment with Charles before he leaves."

Martin nodded his head, then turned to Charles. "You know, regardless of what happens, we're gonna see each other in glory. I can't thank you enough."

The two men shook hands, which then turned into another hug, then Martin walked away into the fog a bit like a cowboy riding off into the sunset until he disappeared over the horizon.

CHAPTER 30

"I saw Ethel earlier," Davy said after Martin left. "She was walking out into the fog. I think she left. I've seen some people leave here by walking away, and some just vanish. I don't know what any of it means, or if it means anything at all. But I think we both know that your time is up here. You've done well, but God wants you to move on to what He has next for you. Like I said, I heard a phone ringing from the cabin earlier and thought it might be worthwhile to see if you could hear your family one more time, but there's no guarantee that they'll answer. It's what I'd do though."

Charles nodded his head in agreement, taking it all in. Part of him knew that he was supposed to rush back to the phone in the cabin, but another part of him couldn't leave without saying goodbye to his friend and mentor. "Davy, it's been so good seeing you again. I can't express how much you've meant to me over the years. It's funny that I went to you for counsel so many times over the years. You were a steady voice who always helped me find the Lord's direction. It's been the same here."

Davy tilted his head slightly and smiled at Charles, obviously taken aback by Charles's kind words. For a moment it looked like he might shed a tear, but he didn't. He looked up as if looking through the fog and into heaven. "You know, Charles, I'm going to be upset if you make it to glory before I do. But if you do, save me a cup of coffee."

"You know I will," Charles replied.

The two men hugged each other, much in the same way that a son would hug his father. No more words were exchanged; none seemed to feel right in this moment. Charles then forced himself to walk back to his cabin one more time. He remembered coming to the phone when he had arrived at Bayou Refuge and being petrified of it, then knowing it meant connection with his family on some level and not wanting to leave it. Still, there was something humbling and a bit frightening in knowing that this may be the last time he got to hear the voices of his family, or wondering if he would even get to hear them. Nothing was guaranteed. He knew he'd see them in glory, but despite being ready on some level to die, his heart still was fighting to hold on to life. The visions he had of his family, of his daughter and son grown, of his grandchildren, of Deborah there at the end of his life weren't likely real, but in some way it made him feel like he had lived a bit of that life. He couldn't imagine feeling any fuller in his heart than if they had been real.

When Charles made his way to the cabin, he walked through the hallway, slowly taking in each step, letting his eyes soak in the fluorescent hallway lights, the wood paneling, and the worn-out carpet. He walked over to his room and stopped before he put his hand on the doorknob.

"God, I'm scared," Charles said. "I know I shouldn't be, but this is hard. Can I please hear their voices one more time?"

Then he turned the doorknob and walked into the room. He looked at his clothes he'd hung in the little closet that he had left open. Charles stared at the picture hanging of a cross standing on an island, remembering the dream he'd had right after he arrived. Just as that cross stood in the center of that island, he knew that no matter what was happening to Him, Christ was at the center of it.

Then he turned his eyes to the phone sitting on the desk, but before he walked over to it, it shook with the vibrations of a ring that seemed like the loudest, most unsettling noise he had ever heard.

CHAPTER 31

"Hello," Charles said as he answered the phone. He felt as if he ought to say more. It seemed like *hello* wasn't enough. But then again, all those years of answering a phone the same way were hard to let go. Then he found himself saying it again after several seconds of not hearing anything. For a moment he felt like the line had gone dead, but then he began to hear the faint beeping and humming of medical equipment. Then he could hear what sounded like the voice of a man speaking, a voice he had heard earlier, the one who had spoken to his wife. Except this time the doctor wasn't speaking to Deborah but to someone else.

"I need you to listen to me closely," the doctor said. "I think there's some movement here, but I've done what I can do. Pastor Charles, do you have any fight left in you?"

"What? I do!" Charles said loudly, although he wasn't sure if the doctor could hear him or not.

"I get a sense there's still some hope, Pastor Charles, but I can't keep you like this long. You know your family won't let you stay in this state. They'll be making some hard choices soon. I understand you're a preacher, not like one of those TV ones but a real preacher who loves his people, teaches them God's Word, and tries to help them. Pastor Charles, I'm sure heaven would be glad to have you, but if the Lord will let you come back for a bit longer, I think we could use you here. I've had some sweet old ladies come up here and pray over you. I've seen men come and anoint your head with oil and cry for their pastor. And there's a sweet woman with two precious children who has hardly left your side.

Charles could hear the words of the doctor and longed to fight. He longed to know what the plan was. He wanted to know if it was in God's will for him to move on to glory or for him to go back home. While in some way he was ready for either one, he longed to be back in that recliner at home with Connor and Shelby picking at each other while Deborah cooked some supper. To look out that big window and watch the squirrels and birds play in the old magnolia tree. He knew it wasn't heaven, but it was the closest he'd been to it so far. But he couldn't understand what it meant to fight. How could he fight for survival in this altered state? What could he do? It felt like he had no options. Then he wondered if it was just his flesh wanting control, or if God was wanting him to hang on and fight, so he could return to his family and his church. In his heart, as strong as the desire was to be with his family, he had finally come to a place where more than being with them, he wanted to please God and be willing to accept whatever the Lord had for him, whether it was returning home or going to glory.

"God, am I missing something?" Charles asked softly. "Show me! What do you want, Lord? I don't know what to do."

Then he heard another voice, one he recognized and had longed to hear. "Is everything okay, Doctor?" Deborah said.

"Well, yes. We're about the same as we have been, some slight fluctuations, but nothing definitive," the doctor replied, then laughed very nervously. "You know, we tell families and friends to talk to their loved ones even when they aren't responsive, but sometimes as doctors we forget to do the same. I try to visit with them some. I've had a few over the years who woke up tell me that they remembered me talking to them. Some could remember what I said word for word."

"What did they say it's like?" Charles heard Deborah ask. "Being in a coma like Charles is."

"Well, it's different for different people. Some don't remember a thing; it was like they took a long nap. Their memory goes from the event that caused the coma to waking up. Others remember bits and pieces of people talking to them. Some talk about dreams that they had. I've had some tell me they remember feeling certain things or seeing people or going places. Most have a hard time explaining it. Some want to talk about it; others don't. For some, little pieces of dreams or things they heard people in the hospital say will come back to them over the years."

"Is it peaceful?" Deborah asked.

"It usually is. Especially if the patient isn't in a lot of pain."

"Thanks for all you've done, Doctor. The kids and I appreciate it more than you know."

"It's my privilege to use the gifts God has given me," the doctor replied. "I'm going to let you spend some time with your husband now. And like we talked about earlier, in the morning we can see where we are and discuss what things need to be considered moving forward."

Charles could hear the door open and close and could feel pressure on his hand as if it were being squeezed. There was a sense of love and calm that swept over him so heavily that he felt like it would overtake him. "Charles," Deborah started. "Everything is kind of confusing right now. I can deal with you dying if the Lord is ready to take you, but I don't want to make the wrong decision. This has always been my biggest fear, but I know even in my fear that the Lord is with me and will walk me through this. I just don't want the kids to wonder if I did enough. I know I'll be all right, but this is a lot. I don't want to do life without you if I don't have to. I've prayed and I've wept and I've struggled. I know this is selfish, but I've asked God this and I'm going to ask you the same thing one more time, and I know the two of you will know what to do."

As she spoke it was as if she had leaned into his ear and whispered, "Will you come back home?"

The words shot a spark through his body. As he sat in the chair by the phone, he could feel his body and soul being stirred, being shook from its core. An overwhelming realization came over him, even stronger than before, that his time at Bayou Refuge was over. It was now time for him to leave, and there was only one way that he could think to do that.

So he hung up the phone, grabbed his car keys off the dresser, and made his way out the door, not sure of where he was going but very eager to face the journey.

CHAPTER 32

Charles knew in his mind that this didn't make sense. In this reality it seemed as if he was brought here and was stuck and there was no way out. The fog was like the bars of a cell keeping him from leaving. He knew there was no guarantee that his car would be there, much less start or actually take him anywhere. There was a real chance that even if it did, he could drive around for hours and wind up right back here at Bayou Refuge, or worse, lost somewhere in the fog. However, he knew in his core that his time here was done. He'd had his conversations. He didn't know what other purpose there was in staying, so perhaps leaving was the only way to fight, to get back home, or—if the Lord willed it—to get into glory.

This feeling, this urgency trumped any fear or hesitation in the face of his uncertainty and superseded the desire to stay and soak in any of the nostalgia offered by Bayou Refuge. Charles also didn't feel any urge to tarry. He had always been like that. It had aggravated Deborah some over the years. When a trip was over, when vacation was done, when an event was finished, it was time to head out. This, he felt, was no different. He walked briskly, still in his dress clothes. It felt strange that he had left his bags behind, but in his haste to leave he hadn't thought of them until this moment. Regardless of where he was going, he wouldn't need them. Still, it did feel strange to leave with nothing, here he was on what was probably the most important trip of his life and he couldn't take anything with him. The swampy air felt somewhat lighter, and the fog seemed less heavy, like it might be clearing. Charles's eyes couldn't help but look up into the cypress trees as he walked. He was almost convinced that for a second he was able to see to the top of one of them. Then he glanced out onto the old bayou, the farthest he had since he arrived. He was almost certain he could make out a little island in the marsh with the cross on it, like the picture in his cabin. Somehow this encouraged him, reinforced in him that he was doing the right thing.

As he continued the walk, he attempted to count the days he had been here. He came to reason that it was probably for a weekend, but for the life of him he couldn't figure out how long it had really been. It seemed like it had only been a few days, but in some ways it felt longer than a weekend. Maybe it had been a week, or had it? His mind struggled to figure out exactly when he had arrived and what day of the week it was right now. Then he wondered if time worked here in this place the same as it did in the real world. This line of thought made his brain hurt so he tried to clear his mind and focus on what he was about to do.

As he walked around the welcome center, he noticed that the road out of the camp seemed to be clearing. He could see maybe fifty yards out just as the fog around the rest of the camp had lifted some. He could only take this as a sign. The second thing Charles saw was Claude in his blue overalls standing next to his car. This sight cause Charles to slow down a bit and walk to his car at a more relaxed pace, not wanting to make the older man feel like Charles was so eager to leave that he wouldn't miss him or even stop to say goodbye.

"I guess you're heading out," Claude said as Charles approached.

"Claude, I think my time here is done," Charles said, feeling bad about leaving Claude behind.

"I think she went on," Claude said, then turned his face to avoid looking at Charles. "She was real excited about having you come here again and lead a Seekers Weekend, just like the old times. Maybe this was it. Maybe this was all the Lord wanted from her."

"What are you going to do?" Charles asked.

"I don't know," Claude said, looking back at Charles again, taking his time with his words. "I feel like Davy and I probably still have some purpose for being here. I guess until the Lord comes and gets us, we just have to seek, trust, and wait. You know this ain't the end though."

Charles wasn't really sure what Claude meant, and perhaps the confusion in his eyes was enough to let Claude know he didn't understand. "We'll see each other again one way or another. I'm sure we'll eat some of whatever Ethel and them angels fix in glory."

The thought of Ethel cooking in heaven made Charles smile. Claude reached out to shake Charles's hand, and they both nodded their heads in agreement. "Take care of yourself, Claude. I'm looking forward to that day."

Claude slowly moved away from the vehicle. Charles threw his bags in the back seat, then sat in the driver's seat and closed the door behind him. As he buckled his seatbelt, he prayed to the Lord that this was the right thing to do. As he turned the ignition, the car started with just a bit of hesitation, making Charles wonder for a minute if this was a futile effort. However, once he backed out and turned toward the road leading out of Bayou Refuge, he was convinced again that this was the right plan. As he drove down the road, although the fog to his left and right remained thick, the fog in front of him seemed to continually break, showing the road in front of him. However, when he tried to look back at Bayou Refuge from the rearview mirror, it was as if it didn't even exist. A blanket of fog resettled in a seemingly supernatural way, keeping Charles from seeing the camp. Then the road began to descend, so even if the fog behind him broke, he wouldn't be able to see the camp.

He guessed there was no point in looking back anymore. There was only one thing to do in Charles's mind: keep driving forward.

CHAPTER 33

The dirt road continued for a while, and everything looked as he had remembered it. Then it switched to a paved road, and after what seemed like several minutes, he arrived back at the stop sign that turned back onto the main road. Charles hesitated for a moment. Suddenly his surroundings didn't look so familiar. Even though he had made the drive countless times, this time he felt lost, unsure of which way to turn. It would have been hard for him to describe, but somehow in his core, he felt like which direction he went was a big deal.

The road gave him the option to turn left, right, or to stay straight. His gut instinct was to turn left. However, he was struggling a bit with trusting that instinct. Part of him thought that even though this place looked like somewhere he had been before, it really wasn't. This Bayou Refuge had not been the same one he had spent all that time in over the years. It was merely something God had placed in this reality to give him and those around him a sense of comfort and peace. So by that logic, turning left wasn't necessarily going to take him back home. Although in his mind he thought it was the way that he had come here. There still was no guarantee that everything was fixed here. A road that took him one place at one time here may not take him back to the same place. In fact, what he needed to get home was to somehow get out of this whole reality. The thought of all of it made his brain hurt.

Not knowing what else to do, he put the car in neutral, got out, and took a few steps toward the intersection. He looked to the left and could make out the road and a small grassy shoulder on both sides with the beginnings of a ditch just beyond the shoulders. He looked to the right and saw just about the same thing except it looked like there might have been some sort of building just at the edge of where the fog made it too hard to see. Then he looked in front of him and saw that the road began to slope up and go over a train track. He stared at the track and thought for a moment. He remembered this track. Part of him had always wondered where the road headed to over the tracks. In fact, he had always planned, when coming to Bayou Refuge, to keep going down that road when he headed back home but had always talked himself out it. There was always a reason to get back the more certain way.

"God, I don't know what to do!" Charles called out. "I really want to wake up and see my wife and kids. I love being a pastor, God. I'd like to keep doing that some more, but You're in control. I'll do whatever You want. But either way, I'm ready to leave this place. You've gotten me this far. Will You show me the way?"

Charles wasn't sure what kind of answer he was expecting, probably more of a feeling or some sort of insight. As he looked around, though, he had no more clarity than before he prayed. He felt like getting in the vehicle and going the way he had always gone, at least the way he thought he remembered going, which was left. However, his heart was unsettled in that. He stood there, staring at his black dress shoes in the dirt. Then he looked back at the old vehicle. He thought about how he should have taken his family's advice and gotten a new phone or at least a new charger. His mind flashed back to all those times over the years that Davy had told him that he needed truck instead of a car. Perhaps a truck would have handled the accident better. However, there was no point in dwelling on those regrets. So he did his best to clear his head and then he looked at the road to the left, then the right, and finally right in front of him. As he looked at the train tracks, he caught the faintest outline of a long tree limb laying on the ground right up against the tracks. It looked familiar, but he couldn't figure out why at first? As he followed the dips and knots of the downed limb, he recognized it as the one he had seen on the road after his accident, the one he had hit.

"Wait a second," Charles said to himself. "I hit you, so why are you right there?"

Was this it? Was this the sign or the direction he had asked God to provide? The reality was that this was all he had to go on, and there seemed to be a peace and general curiosity in him that came from somewhere just to go straight. So he got back in the car and started it back up for what he hoped would be the last time. Then out of habit, he checked both ways, even though he knew no one was coming. Charles drove straight, going up the slope and over the railroad tracks, the car vibrating slightly as he crossed over them.

CHAPTER 34

Charles wasn't sure what he was expecting to see as he crossed over the tracks, but he was expecting *something* to happen and he wasn't wrong. As soon as he crossed over the tracks and came down the small hill, the fog was replaced with total darkness. Then he had the feeling of free-falling. As best he figured, he was no longer in the vehicle but plummeting through the air with his back facing the ground, if there was any ground below him to hit when he landed. There wasn't anything he could do to stop it or slow it down, so he just went with it, trying to pretend in his mind that he was on a roller coaster or skydiving to keep from being driven crazy by the sensation. This seemed to go on for what felt like forever. Charles didn't know whether his eyes were open or closed; everything was so dark, like he was falling down a black tube. The sensation seemed to grow more and more intense with Charles wondering if this is what the actual process of dying felt like. If it was, he hoped it would end quickly. Charles also wondered, for a brief second, if he should be concerned with the fact that he was going down and not up. He knew deep down it didn't mean anything bad, but he couldn't deny the oddness of it. However, he had never felt anything quite like this before and was convinced that this was the end. God must be calling him home. His body was giving out, and his soul would soon be in glory.

He tried to thank God for everything: his parents, his wonderful wife, his children, and the men who had equipped him for ministry over the years. However, the sensation, the intensity of free-falling made it hard to focus on much else. All he could do was endure it.

Then it happened. The feeling of falling was interrupted by the feeling of an earth-shattering stop; his whole being was shaken. There wasn't an explosion of pain like he expected though. In fact, at first he didn't feel anything at all, but slowly his entire body did begin to ache. It took an act of Congress for him to move his fingers or his toes. He couldn't even lift his leg up; it felt like it weighed a ton. He tried to open his mouth, but his throat felt raw, strange. What was happening? Why did he feel this way? He racked his brain to understand what was going on. His mind felt odd; he became very confused all of a sudden. Then he remembered something about a tree limb on the way to a meeting. Had he hit a limb? Had he swerved and missed running into something else? Suddenly, he couldn't remember. Charles also had the sensation that he had been somewhere else after that, but it wasn't clear.

Charles could feel his hand tightening, being squeezed. He realized that his eyes were closed, so he went to open them. They wouldn't budge much. As he attempted to open them again, a speck of light came through, but only for a second. With a concerted effort he focused all his attention on his eyes, like a child trying to make themselves wake up in the middle of a bad dream, and then the light broke through. It was blinding, and the sensation of air on his eyes was odd and almost overpowering. He squinted and tried to adjust. It took him a second to realize he was in a dark room lit only by a lamp and a television screen. Where was he?

Though the place seemed pretty quiet with only some light beeping and humming noises, it felt like there were walls around him. On the other side of those walls he could hear people talking, something with wheels being moved and a door being closed. Charles wanted to turn his head, and while he could move it slightly, it ached to move it more than an inch or two. Plus, there was this thing that he could see coming out of his mouth. His hand still felt squeezed.

However, despite how limited the movement he made was, it stirred something next to him. The squeezing of his hand stopped, and then he saw a beautiful face standing over him.

"You're awake!" Deborah said. "Praise God, you're awake!"

CHAPTER 35

Tears filled his eyes as he looked at his beautiful wife. His mind was trying solve the mystery of why he was here, however, as his eyes gazed upon his wife his mind just focused on her. He wanted to say something but couldn't. All he could do was muster enough strength to squeeze Deborah's hand. Charles tried to blink the tears away. It felt like he had been away from her forever. His heart ached in some way as if he had never expected to see her again in this life. He couldn't describe the feeling; it was too strange. But there she was in her favorite green top. And even though he couldn't turn his head, he knew she had blue jeans and sandals on like she almost always did. Her hair looked like she hadn't washed it in several days, and her eyes gave him the impression that she'd been crying and hadn't gotten much sleep. In Charles's heart, he was so glad to see her, but the missing pieces of the puzzle were confusing him. Once again his mind turned back to the mystery of this moment.

What had happened? Why was he here? Charles felt like he was forgetting something important. Then he remembered Connor urging him to get a new phone. Deborah being upset with him because the fog was thick. He recalled driving to the meeting, then nothing—except waking up and being in this moment. His heart ached as he thought about what this meant. Deborah was right. He should have stayed home. It seemed he had caused so much pain because he didn't listen, because he wanted to be in control.

Maybe because they had been together so long that she knew what he'd be thinking, or maybe it was just because it was the logical thing to do, Deborah began to address his confusion.

"Five days ago you were on your way to the meeting," she said as she wiped a tear from her eye. "And it seems like a large tree limb was laying on the edge of the road. You hit it, managing to flip the car over ,and you landed in the ditch. It knocked you unconscious, and you took some brain damage. We didn't know if you were going to wake up or not. Your brain just wasn't coming back like it needed to."

She stopped and turned her head, no doubt not wanting him to see more tears falling from her eyes. He squeezed her hand as tight as he could, and after a few seconds she turned her head back around and looked him in the eyes. "I was so mad at you that morning, and I just let you leave without telling you I loved you. I'm sorry. We thought we lost you. I thought you were gone. I prayed and prayed, and the kids and the church prayed. God is so good. I'm so glad you're back."

They just stared at each other for a moment, not needing any words, glad to be together, knowing that they had more time with each other. Charles's heart was full. He couldn't imagine wanting anything other than more time with his wife and children. He knew in his heart where he would have gone if he had died, but he wasn't ready yet. He wanted to see his kids grow up, see them get married and have grandchildren, and he wanted to grow old with his wife. If the Lord let him, he wanted to preach and pastor his little church until the Lord called him home. He was glad to be here, to be alive, to have more time on this side of life, even with as much as his body ached and as much as it felt like he was forgetting something important.

CHAPTER 36

The first few days were very emotional. Within several hours of waking up, they took the tube out and Charles could speak again. However, his throat was dry, and his strength was so limited that he couldn't get out very much. He smiled and squeezed hands and cried with both of his children. All of the deacons from the church showed up and encouraged him, letting him know that the church would be all right; he'd have all the time in the world he'd need to recover. Friends and extended family called and talked to him on the phone. Deborah, Connor, or Shelby held the phone to his ear, and he'd listen and smile as people expressed their joy at knowing he was awake and, according to the doctors, should recover fully, despite having a long road ahead.

Each day it seemed like he gained a little more strength. He could sit up longer, move his arms, legs, and turn his head a little more than he could the day before. When the physical therapist came by, he'd spend an hour working all the different parts of his body and giving him simple exercises that he could do from his hospital bed to help him regain strength. It was their plan to have him out of the bed and doing some walking by the end of the week. Usually by the time they left, Charles was worn out and all he wanted to do was sleep.

After a particularly challenging session he took a long nap, and when he woke up he saw Connor sitting in the hospital chair, fiddling with the television remote while eating a candy bar.

"Always eating something," Charles said, glad to hear some strength and volume coming back to his voice.

"Hey, taking care of you is hard work," Connor said with a smile.

"Yeah, you look like you're really working over there," Charles replied with a laugh. "Where's your mom and Shelby?"

"She said she had to run a few errands, and Shelby went with her. They'll be back in a bit."

The two sat for a moment as Connor flipped through channels. There was nothing on but talk shows, soap operas, and reruns. Charles's mind began to wonder about everything that had happened and the realization that he didn't really know how much time had passed since the accident. "Connor?"

"Yeah, Dad."

"Remind me again, how long was I out?"

"Five days, Dad," Connor replied. "The longest five days of my life."

"I'm sorry. I can't imagine how hard that must have been for you. I lost my dad after I had grown up and it was still really hard."

"Dad?" Connor said in a way that indicated he had a question.

"Yeah, bud."

"What was it like being out like that? You know, in the coma? Do you remember anything?" Connor asked.

"Hmm," Charles said as he thought about it. He really didn't remember much. It seemed like he remembered the vehicle shaking or hitting something. He felt like he had been somewhere. It was a strange feeling, like he had gone on a trip or done something important while he was out. Of course, it had to have been a dream. Then there was a feeling of intense falling and then waking up. Then at that moment something else hit him, something he was certain happened. "I don't remember much. I think I remember the accident, then just feelings like you get after you wake from a dream that you can't remember. I think I remember hearing you guys talk to me: you, your sister and your mom. You guys telling me it was okay and that you were praying for me and wanted me to wake up, but—"

Charles had to stop for a second and get his composure. "But telling me it'd be okay if I didn't and if I went on to heaven."

Connor, still in the chair, looked down to avoid eye contact with his dad. Charles knew it had to be to avoid showing tears. After a few seconds Connor spoke without looking at his dad. "We'd have been okay. You've showed us what it means to know Jesus and to love others. I'd have taken care of mom, but I'm sure glad you didn't."

"Me too," Charles said. "Me too."

Later that afternoon, Deborah sat in the room with him while Shelby and Connor went to walk around the hospital and stretch their legs. In the back of Charles's mind, he figured they were visiting the vending machine as well. Deborah was working on a crossword puzzle when she looked up from the puzzle and over at Charles who was deep in thought.

"You'll never guess who I saw down in the cafeteria this morning. I forgot to tell you earlier."

"Who?" Charles asked with an expression that indicated he was glad to have his thoughts interrupted.

"I saw Martha, the wife of Davy, your old ministry director."

"Really?" Charles said, then unexpectedly a wave of emotion hit him. It didn't really make sense though. He hadn't seen Davy in a long time. The last time he saw him he wasn't even sure if Davy recognized who he was. Davy had poured so much into Charles's ministry. He had always been a constant source of encouragement and someone who would listen to him, share the truth with him even when he didn't want to hear it, and encourage him when Charles had felt like ministry had gotten the best of him. Charles had to fight the sudden, unexplainable urge to cry. "Precious people."

Deborah looked at Charles and could tell he was struggling. "You okay?"

"Yeah, yeah," Charles replied. "I'm fine. All this medicine just has my emotions out of whack. Did she say how Davy was doing?"

"Well, actually he's here in the hospital. He fell and hurt himself pretty good. They had to do surgery. He'll be here another day or two. She says he's out of it most of the time. Like he's staring off into space. But she'd love for you to come and pray with him if you feel like getting over there, but she'd understand if you don't."

"I think I'd like that. It'd be good to see him again even if he doesn't recognize me."

The two sat in silence for a moment. Charles's mind shifted to something he felt like he needed to say but was having trouble getting the words together. He knew it shouldn't be this difficult, but pride was a tough thing. Charles wasn't as afraid of saying the words as he was the emotions he'd have to fight back. The loud closing of a door down the hallway startled him. As he turned on instinct toward the entrance to the room, he met Deborah's eyes, which were fixed intently on him.

"What is wrong?" she asked calmly but deliberately. "I know when something is wrong with my husband.

Charles looked down at the thin blue sheet covering his legs. "Give me a second." Charles replied as he forced himself to look Deborah in the eyes.

"I'm not going anywhere," Deborah replied with a slight smile to try and ease the moment.

"I didn't listen to you that morning, and I should have," Charles began directly. As tears began to appear in Deborah's eyes, he cleared his throat and continued with a much softer voice. "Deborah, it was disrespectful of me not to consider what you were saying and to take it more seriously. My stubbornness caused you and the kids a lot of pain."

Deborah grabbed a tissue and wiped her eyes. "Dad left us. That was so hard, and I watched Mom struggle. While you were out, my mind kept going back to watching her try to hold things together. I was mad at you! But as I sat and prayed and talked to you, I knew in my heart this was different. You made a mistake, a bad choice out of a good intention. God let me know in my heart that I was going to be okay. I will forgive you for not listening to me if you'll forgive me for letting you leave without kissing you back or saying *I love you*."

"I knew you loved me. It was just a bad morning," Charles said. He felt relief from addressing the issue. "God blessed me with a wise wife and some pretty intelligent kids, and I think I'm going to try harder to listen to what they have to say from here on out."

"I think, Charles Grey," Deborah said with a laugh as she wiped her eyes, "that you knowing that makes you a wise man."

"Hey, on the plus side, I get a new car," Charles said with a large grin.

"Something with updated safety features," Deborah said emphatically.

"Probably not a bad idea. I guess I might need to get a new phone too."

"Connor has already picked one out for you," Deborah replied with a smile as she grabbed Charles's hand.

Two days later the physical therapist had Charles up and walking. It was definitely hard work. He thought that if any of his church members saw him struggling, they might think he was drunk. The thought of that made him laugh. The therapist had him walking holding a wooden support connected to the wall of the hospital hall. Shelby walked at her father's side, holding his side and his hand. Charles figured she was going to try to keep him from falling. However, he wasn't so sure that he wouldn't pull both of them down if he fell. She was as stubborn as he was and wasn't going to listen to reason. Plus, the physical therapist was walking right behind Charles, pushing a wheelchair just in case he couldn't go any farther.

"You ready to turn back?" the therapist asked Charles.

"I got a little more in me," Charles said. "Can we walk over to the waiting area just up ahead? I need to take care of my assistant here. I see some vending machines."

"That sounds like a good plan," the therapist replied.

Charles looked over to Shelby, almost slipping as he did. She smiled at him and said, "Careful, Daddy. I think you just want a bag of chips."

"Well . . ." Charles replied with a smirk. "It would be rude of me to let you eat alone."

Charles was finally starting to get his appetite back. Though he couldn't eat much at one time, his body wanted him to eat often, so he'd been snacking throughout the day. It was a bad habit he knew he'd have to break when he got home. As they came up to the waiting area, there were about a dozen wooden chairs with red cushions on the seat bottoms and backs. Along the wall next to a large window were a few vending machines. One for coffee, one for snacks, and another for drinks.

"You got my card, Shelby?" Charles asked.

"Yes, Daddy."

"Well get me some potato chips, and get whatever you and our friend here need," he said as he looked over at his therapist.

"I'm good. Why don't you take a seat for a minute and catch your breath," the therapist replied. "I'll check in at the nurses' station, then come right back."

As Charles sat down in the wheelchair, he realized that someone was in one of the chairs next to him. A man with dirty-blond hair wearing hospital gown with a brown leather jacket over the gown. The man had a book in his hands, which Charles quickly realized was a Bible. It was something Charles liked to see, but what threw him off was that the man was looking at him. He stared a way that someone looks at someone they recognize but can't figure out how. The man didn't avert his eyes when he saw that Charles knew he was staring at him but continued. Initially, this made Charles uncomfortable. However, after a few seconds Charles couldn't shake the feeling that he had also seen the man before.

Charles, not knowing what else to do, decided to break the ice. "What are you in for?"

Even though Charles wasn't looking at Shelby, he knew she'd be nodding her head in embarrassment at her dad's lame joke. Still, jokes, even when lame, helped to disarm people.

"Drugs, believe it or not," the man replied.

"Oh, I'm sorry to hear that," Charles replied. "That's a good book you got there."

The man broke eye contact with Charles to look down at his blue Gideon Bible. "Yeah, grew up on this stuff. Saw some bad things in church and kind of turned my back on it. Seems like I was looking at it the wrong way though."

"What made you turn back to it?"

"When I was out, I thought I was going to die. I had some sort of experience I can't get my head around. Can't even remember all of it, but I'll just say that when I woke up, I knew I had I quit running from God. So I decided to run to Him. By the way, you look so familiar."

"You do too," Charles said. "I'm a pastor. Maybe we ran into each other somewhere along the way."

"No, that's not it," the man replied. "I'm not from around here, and I don't think we'd have been running in the same circles."

"Hmm," Charles said. "Well, I guess it's just one of those mysteries. What's your name? I'd like to be able to pray for you."

"Tristan," the man responded. Charles had never felt so certain that he had met someone who was a complete stranger. However, he had no way of placing where he had seen the man or what was happening when he did. Maybe it was just the meds the doctors had given him.

"Well, Tristan, I'm Charles. I'll be praying for you. I can help you find a church and some help with your recovery if you need it."

"I appreciate that," Tristan responded. "I'll be going back home though. I've got some connections there that I've talked to that are going to help me. But I'll take all the prayers I can get."

Charles nodded in acknowledgment. At that point Shelby walked over with his snack and the therapist came back and was motioning for Charles to stand. As Charles stood, he looked over at Tristan one more time. "Nice to meet you."

"Same here," Tristan replied.

Charles slowly walked back to the room. As he did, he glanced at an open hospital door where a crew of doctors and nurses had just arrived with a crash cart. A middle-age man was standing next to the bed, crying.

"Come on, Kayla!" the man said. "Not like this."

Charles said a prayer as he walked by, asking for God's help in the situation. It was only God's grace that kept him from being the one who left a spouse behind.

CHAPTER 37

The next day Charles received quite a surprise. A home nurse and physical therapist had been lined up by the hospital and his insurance. The nurse and physical therapist would be making several visits to his house each week to make sure that his recovery was going as planned. However, the doctors felt like the best place for him to continue his recovery was at home.

"You know, it's going to take them a while to process the paperwork, so there's no point in getting in a rush," Deborah told him.

"Yeah, I agree," he said as he sat in a chair next to the bed eating a bowl of grits, his breakfast that morning. "I'd like to go see Davy and Martha if they're still here."

"We can do that. I think it would mean the world to Martha. And who knows, maybe Davy will recognize you," Deborah replied. "Finish your breakfast and we can go over that way. It's one floor down. I have the room number."

Charles finished his breakfast while halfway looking at the birds out of the window and watching the local morning news. The newscaster was referencing a *Dateline* special about a young boy who had attracted media coverage because of a rare disorder he was born with, one that caused him to sleep for long periods of time and left him in a wheelchair, largely unresponsive to the world around him. The young boy's parents had fought with insurance companies to continue to provide medical support to those in similar situations. A reporter showed pictures of the child lying in a bed next to his family. They called the young boy Kenny. Apparently, he had passed away recently.

Then the reporter switched to a story about an owner of a chain of grocery stores in New Orleans who had also passed away. Martin something or another. The man looked familiar. Charles then remembered that way back in seminary he had worked for a company that sold phone systems. He had some grocery stores that were clients and had seen the owner's face on advertisements as well as seeing him in the store a time or two. Once he finished his grits, he washed them down with the last of his coffee. The hospital coffee was a chore to get down. He loved drinking a fresh cup of black coffee, but this hospital concoction needed a little something to make it palatable. A little cream helped just enough to make it bearable and almost enjoyable.

Deborah pushed him in the wheelchair because he wanted to save his strength for physical therapy, which he was hoping he would still have today before he left the hospital. It was a short roll down the white-tiled hallway to the elevator and then just down the hall one floor below.

"Room 3215," Deborah said as they stopped at a door. "This is it. Let me knock to make sure they're up for company."

As Deborah tapped on the door, a voice on the inside shouted out, "Come on in!"

Deborah opened the door and Charles reached out his foot to push it forward the rest of the way. They came into the room and Charles could see Martha sitting in a wooden chair with a blue cushion next to the bed. She was wearing a striped blue top and white pants, and her white hair was fixed perfectly. Like many older Southern women, she was going to make sure she was presentable no matter where she was.

"Look, Davy," Martha said to her husband. "We have some company."

Davy lay in the bed in a grey hospital gown just like Charles's. His once-large frame seemed diminished. His grey hair had thinned out even more than the last time Charles had seen him, and it looked like he hadn't been eating well. His left arm rested on the side of the bed and was covered in bruises from his fall. It looked like there was some bruising on the left side of his face as well. Even though Martha had spoken to him, the man expressed no indication by word or in nonverbal communication that he had heard a word.

"Hey, Davy," Charles said as Deborah rolled him up next to the bed. "It's Charles. It's good to see you."

Davy didn't respond. Charles wasn't expecting him to, but he'd be lying if he said he didn't want his old friend and mentor to remember and recognize him. Deborah put a hand on Charles's shoulder, her own subtle way of comforting her husband. Charles appreciated it.

"This is how it's been lately," Martha said. She stood and rubbed Davy's cheek. "Baby, our friends are here. They love you and wanted to say hello."

Davy responded just a little to her touch and gave a slight change in his expression, but only for a few seconds, then his eyes returned to a vacant stare. Martha turned and looked at Deborah and Charles. "It's hard. He still has occasional moments where he's with me, talking with me. Sometimes it makes sense; most of the time it seems like he's confused. He was having one of those confused moments when he fell. Probably about a week ago. In fact, it was the same day you got in your wreck, Charles. Anyway, he got out of his chair, saying something about Bayou Refuge, that old church camp we used to have events at. You remember those retreats and Seeker weekends?"

"Hmm," Charles said. An odd emotion swept over him at the mention of that place, like a sense of peace. "Yes, I have a lot of memories of that old place."

"Oh yeah," Deborah said. "We had some great times there. God really used that old retreat center. Say, how's old Claude and his wife Ethel doing? Whatever happened to them when the place shut down?"

"Funny you should mention that," Martha replied. "They've both been in a nursing facility. Her niece helped them get situated there. Been there for several years now. Both have dementia like

Davy. Well, I should say *had.* I got word yesterday that Ethel had actually passed away. Man, that woman loved the Lord and could cook."

The thought of Ethel's cooking made Charles smile. The couple had always been gracious hosts to Charles and the other pastors as well as everyone who went to Bayou Refuge. He was sad that she had passed away, but glad that she wasn't suffering anymore. Charles's mind turned back to his friend in the hospital bed. He grabbed the railing next to Martha and began to stand.

"Honey, do you need help?" Deborah asked. "Please, be careful."

"No, I'm good," Charles said. It took him a few seconds to get his balance good. Once he had it, he looked Davy in the eyes, and they actually focused a bit on Charles. Like he was trying to process something. Then Davy slowly smiled, showing his teeth, grinning like a small child.

"Oh, praise the Lord," Martha said. "I think he knows who you are."

"You're back," the old man said slowly and with a bit of a slur. "You're back."

"Yeah, brother. I'm back here with you," Charles replied, not sure what the old man was trying to say. "I sure do miss having you around."

"We got together . . . at the Refuge," Davy said in a raspy voice, then he lifted his hand and placed it over Charles's. "It was good."

"Yeah, we had a lot of good times over the years at the Refuge," Charles said.

"I'm so proud of you. You did so good," Davy told him as he squeezed his hand.

Charles had a distinct feeling that the old man knew exactly what he was talking about and was trying to tell Charles something, but he dismissed that and simply appreciated that Davy was proud of him. The words warmed his heart in a special way. Davy and Charles smiled at each other, then Davy, with a total sense of peace, closed his eyes and fell asleep. Charles prayed for Martha and Davy, then he and Deborah hugged the elderly woman and said their goodbyes.

EPILOGUE

ONE YEAR LATER

Charles walked in the wooden door of his house, set his computer bag by his recliner, and went into the kitchen to grab a glass of water. He knew that Connor would be at baseball practice, and Deborah had to run a couple of errands after picking up Shelby from school and dropping her off here to do her homework.

"Hey, Dad!" Shelby called from the kitchen table as he walked to the cabinet to grab a cup.

"Hey, Shelby! Getting that homework knocked out?"

"You know it," she replied without looking up from her computer. "Hey, a package came for you. It's on the counter."

"Thanks," Charles replied. "Who's it from?"

"Mrs. Martha. That lady you and mom know," Shelby responded.

Charles walked over to the counter and saw a long, thin box. It was obvious that some sort of picture or mirror would probably be the only thing that would fit in it. Charles took his pocketknife out and cut the tape to open the package. When he got it open, he pulled out a couple of sheets of brown packing paper, and a piece of paper with some writing on it managed to fall onto the counter. It was a handwritten note with beautiful penmanship.

Hey Charles and Deborah,

Hope you guys are doing well. Davy and I are still hanging in there. Not much has changed. He's experiencing a slow but steady decline. We've moved into an apartment at an assisted living community where I'll have help in taking care of Davy. It's hard, but it's going to be a good thing in the end. In the process of downsizing, I came across this old picture from Bayou Refuge that Davy brought home five years ago when they were clearing out the rooms in hopes of selling the place. I knew that you guys had special ties to the camp, so I figured you might be able to give it a good home.

Keep us in your prayers!

Love y'all,

Martha

"What is it, Dad?" Shelby asked.

"A picture," Charles said as he slowly pulled the painting out of the box. Once it was out, he admired the old wooden frame, rubbing his fingers across it. Then he studied the picture. It was a picture of a little island in the marsh and the sun was setting. In the middle of the island was an old wooden cross. He had seen this before, perhaps at Bayou Refuge, but also in his dreams on occasion. As he looked at the image, he couldn't help but think of God's faithfulness to him and his family while he was in a coma and feel encouraged to know that even in the hard moments of life, God is working, often in ways that we cannot understand.

One Last Thing

I wanted to personally thank you for taking the time to read my book. I know there's a lot to do and a lot to read out there, so it means something to me that you allowed me to share my story with you. I have three personal requests. Since we are not guaranteed any more time in this life, and there's nothing in the Bible that speaks of a final opportunity given, like the one Tristan, Kayla, and Martin had, please take a minute and make sure that your heart is right with the Lord and that you've placed your faith and trust for salvation in Jesus and His work on the cross. If you haven't, let me invite you to pray, committing to turn from your sins, asking to receive what Jesus did on the cross for you for the forgiveness of your sins, and ask Jesus to be the Lord of your life. There's nothing greater than knowing He has your heart and life.

Also, if this book was enjoyable, please take a minute to rate it on Amazon. Every positive review helps others to be able to find and enjoy it. You may know someone else who would enjoy it, so consider buying them a copy or telling them about it.

Finally, please check out my Facebook Page <u>Joshua Powell: Author Page | Facebook</u>. I keep it up to date with free resources, information on upcoming releases, as well as other encouraging content. Thank you again.

Check out *The Edge*, the first novella in Joshua Powell's Stories of Hope series.

Craig Brown wants to move on with his life, but he can't escape The Edge—a seedy bar on the edge of town where he was the night his life fell apart. Every time he closes his eyes, Craig finds himself transported back there. As he struggles to confront what happened that night and watches his life spiral out of control, Craig must choose between remaining trapped by regret or reaching for the hope he no longer believes he deserves.

The Edge is a moving story of grief, healing, and second chances—a reminder that sometimes the road to redemption begins when we reach out to God so we can face the struggles we can't overcome on our own.

Available now on Amazon in paperback, ebook, on Kindle Unlimited and as an Audiobook. Come Visit *The Edge*.

STORIES OF HOPE NOVELLA #1
THE
EDGE
A STORY OF
GRIEF, GRIT, AND GRACE
The EDGE.
Edge
SOME PLACES WON'T LET GO.
SOME MEMORIES WON'T FADE.
JOSHUA POWELL
STORIES OF HOPE